Pride Publishing books by Ann Marie James

Everyone's Mechanic
Chasing the Dream

I0570648

Everyone's Mechanic

CHASING THE DREAM

ANN MARIE JAMES

Chasing the Dream
ISBN # 978-1-83943-805-9
©Copyright Ann Marie James 2019
Cover Art by Erin Dameron-Hill ©Copyright October 2019
Interior text design by Claire Siemaszkiewicz
Pride Publishing

CHASING THE DREAM

Dedication

A huge thank you to my family for their unending support and to Katie and Trampas for encouraging me to keep following the dream of becoming a writer.

Chapter One

Lee stepped into the busy garage and heard the familiar sounds of mechanics hard at work. Having grown up hanging out in, then working, in his father's auto shop since he was fifteen, the sounds meant home to him. Looking around, Lee realized that the similarities between the two businesses ended there. This was the most organized space he had ever seen. There were toolboxes and workstations kept meticulously, with all the tools in their apparent slots when not in use. He'd heard the new owner of Everyone's Mechanic ran a tight ship. The rumor mill had obviously nailed that one. He hoped the rumor mill's claim that the new owner, Kirk Smith, was fantastic to work for was also accurate.

Lee dried his sweaty palms on his pant legs before turning and making his way to the office door that he could see to his left. After he knocked on the doorjamb, the occupant behind the desk looked up at him. A green gaze assessed him from a ruggedly handsome face. *Stop that, idiot. He's your potential boss.* After the man stood up, Lee realized he needed to add 'large' to his description. The man was at least three inches taller than his own six feet. *Wow. Just wow. Down, boy.* Lee hoped his libido would listen to him, because now was *not* the time.

"Hi, I'm Lee Clark. I understand you're looking for a new mechanic?" Lee gestured toward the front window of the shop where a *Help Wanted* sign was posted.

"Yep. I'm Kirk Smith, the new owner of this place." Kirk offered Lee a handshake before sitting back down and waving toward the chair in front of his desk. Lee sat before his shaking knees gave out on him. "What happened there?" Kirk indicated the healing bruises on Lee's face. "You don't have to tell me specifics. I just really need to know if the trouble is going to follow you here."

Lee squared his shoulders, fighting against his normal shyness. He needed this job, but he also wanted to make sure he was going to be safe here too. "My father found out I was gay. He and my brother took exception to it. I worked for my father at his place. Maybe you've heard of it? Clark and Sons?"

Kirk stiffened and Lee prepared himself to get out of there quickly if Kirk made a move toward him.

"Well, we're equal opportunity here. Doesn't matter if you're gay or straight, as long as you can do the job. *Can* you do the job?"

Lee relaxes somewhat.

They were interrupted by someone else knocking on the doorjamb. "Hey, boss man, have you seen the…?" The voice trailed off as he must have realized there was another person in the office with Kirk. "Oh, sorry. I

didn't realize you had someone in here with ya. Wait...
Lee? Is that you, boy?"

Lee relaxed even more as he recognized Will Jackson.
Will had worked for his father once upon a time before
leaving for a better opportunity a little over a year
before. More accurately, Lee's father always had to be
the one in control and didn't like that Will was more
knowledgeable than him. It had made Will's life
difficult. Lee hadn't realized that Will worked here
now. Lee stood and Will came in to give him a hug,
ending it with a manly clap on the back before stepping
away and looking at him more closely.

"Your dad do that to ya?"

"My brother and his friends, actually. Found out I
was gay. Had a problem with it." Surprise, then
understanding crossed Will's features.

"You looking for a job?" Will asked.

"Yes, sir. Dad kicked me out when he found out."

Will turned to Kirk. "You'd be a fool not to hire this
boy. He has mad skills in the garage. He's actually what
has kept Clark and Sons afloat since I left. His loss
would definitely be our gain."

Heat rushed to Lee's face and he just knew he was
blushing. Damn his redheaded pale complexion for
making it obvious that he was flustered. He turned to
look at the man he was hoping would hire him.

"That makes this decision easy. I know how hard you
are to please, old man. Welcome aboard."

"Really?" At Kirk's nod, Lee relaxed fully for the first
time in what felt like forever.

"Hey." Will placed a hand on Lee's shoulder, making
him flinch. He tried to hide the pain but wasn't very
successful. The black eye and facial bruising weren't
the only places he was injured. Will removed his hand

quickly, giving him a serious stare. Lee lowered his head and fixed his gaze on a button of Will's shirt, waiting. Thankfully, Will didn't say anything about it. "Weren't you still living with your dad?"

"Yeah." With a deep sigh, Lee continued, "Everything I own is in my truck out there. I needed to find a place to work first. Now I can find a place to live."

Kirk spoke from his spot behind the desk. "This could work out perfect. The previous owner lived in the apartment above the garage before he died of a heart attack. I didn't know what I was going to do with it. If you want, you can rent it. Then I don't have to worry about the garage at night, since you'll be here." Raising his hand before Lee could say anything, he added, "It's not much, so don't get too excited. It definitely needs some work. I did have it cleaned after I purchased the business from the owner's daughter after he died. The guy was a slob." Kirk grimaced as if that fact pained him, before continuing, "If you take it and want to take on the repairs, I'll pay for the cost of the materials. In exchange, we'll keep the rent reasonable. How's that sound?"

"You would trust me? Just like that?"

"You have Will's recommendation. That's hard to earn. You've had a rough go of it. No sense making drama where there doesn't need to be any. You in?"

"I'm in."

An hour later the paperwork was completed. "Come on now. Let's go show you your new accommodations. As I said, don't expect much. There's an entrance to the side of the building as well as the one there. So, no excuses about your commute." Kirk pointed at the stairs tucked into the corner of the garage. Lee hadn't noticed them behind the large toolboxes.

Lee laughed at the joke, as he was meant to. The metal stairs clanged as they walked up to the fire safety door at the top.

Kirk handed him a key chain with four keys on it. "The silver one opens this door and the door from the outside. The gold opens the front door of the shop. I have no idea what the other two are for. I can't find anything they open downstairs, but I'm afraid to throw them out in case they're important. Maybe they open something in here."

Lee used the silver key to open the door, then stepped into the apartment and got his first look. "Um...wow."

"Yeah. Wow's one word for it."

"You attached to the shag carpeting or are you okay with me ripping it out and maybe putting in a laminate of some kind?" Lee asked.

"Like I said, do what you want. Just give me the receipts as you go, and I'll reimburse you. Anything you do will be an improvement. You haven't even seen the avocado kitchen yet."

"You're kidding."

"Wish I was." Kirk shook his head.

Lee crossed the empty living area to see the kitchen for himself. "Oh my God, you weren't kidding. I don't know what's worse, the avocado appliances or the harvest-gold counters."

"I think the rooster tiles for the backsplash are really what makes it classy," Kirk said.

"This whole thing needs to be gutted."

"Bathroom too. Come on. Let me show you the rest." Kirk waved for Lee to follow.

The rest consisted of a good-size bedroom, a second smaller bedroom and the aforementioned bathroom. Someone had painted the walls a brilliant fuchsia that hurt the eyes when the light fixture was turned on. The cabinet was painted a bright brassy gold color that matched the fixtures on the tub and sink. Ornate did not even begin to describe them.

"Did he just buy whatever was cheapest when he decorated? I can't imagine anyone actually looking for this stuff. This is *bad*." Lee squinted to try to offset some of the glare.

"That was my guess too. He seemingly went with what was deeply discounted or free. One of the guys said he loved to go to garage sales. You should have seen the furniture. I swear the couch disintegrated on the way to the dumpster."

Lee took another look around at the small space. "Holy moly, the tub and toilet are pink. I thought it was a reflection of the paint."

"Oh shit, I didn't realize that either. Well, let me show you the one already good thing about this apartment before you run screaming."

"Just the fact I'll have somewhere to live is a good thing, and I do appreciate it. I won't run screaming. Promise. This is fixable. It's going to take a lot of work, but it's fixable."

"Glad you think so. I just don't have the time to tackle a project like this, between working and my family."

As they were talking, they made their way through the only door they hadn't opened yet on the tour. The door had stairs leading up. Stepping onto the roof, Lee sucked in a breath. One end had a glassed building similar to a greenhouse, with one of those combo heating and air conditioning units, likely to extend the amount of time it could be used. The rest of the space was set up as a barbecue and relaxation area. This had obviously been where the previous owner had spent most of his time. The built-in grill was amazing. The furniture was surprisingly tasteful and of good quality.

Lee turned in a circle, taking in everything. "This is part of it? I can use all this?"

"Yep. Consider it a perk of dealing with the hideousness of the rest of the place."

Lee's brain was spinning. The greenhouse would be perfect for his artwork. He'd been worried about finding a space for it. "It's perfect. Thank you. Thank you so much." They made their way downstairs and back to the kitchen.

"No. Thank *you*. As I said, I don't have the time or the energy to deal with any of this right now. This works out well for both of us. You said all your stuff's in your truck? Want a hand bringing it all in?"

"Oh, I can handle it. I don't want to take up any more of your time." Lee dropped his head to stare at his shoes again. "I don't actually have a whole lot. I have my clothes, my art stuff and my books. I have money to buy things. I was able to save while living at home. It's why I stayed. All I really need is a mattress to start." Lee took another look around. "This place is going to be a construction zone for quite a while."

Kirk took a moment to look around as well. "This is so horrible that I should pay you to live here."

Lee grinned. "I wouldn't be against that, but as long as you can keep my rent reasonable, I can do the work. Well...most of it. Plumbing, not so much. I'll have to get someone in to replace the tub and toilet. I'll need to know a budget."

"We'll work it out. So, you said 'art stuff'. What kind of art do you do?"

Lee ducked his head shyly. "Nothing major. It's just a hobby. Helps me relax."

"Well, you'll certainly need to relax after working on this mess." Kirk made a move as if to pat Lee on the back, causing him to flinch.

"Sorry," Lee said.

"Nothing to be sorry for. Just know that you have nothing to fear anymore. We have your back," Kirk assured him.

"Why would you say that? You just met me."

"You're part of the garage family now. Will speaks highly of you and you haven't run screaming from this mess. That shows strength of character." Kirk smirked as he said the last bit. "Or maybe it's total insanity. Either will fit in here. Come on. Let's get your stuff in."

* * * *

Lee stopped his trip down memory lane as he placed the last subway tile on the backsplash in the kitchen. As he didn't cook much, the kitchen had been the last project he'd tackled. The last three months had been good...very good. As soon as he grouted the backsplash, the renovation would finally be done. He'd settled in well with the other guys in the garage, had a space all his own and was able to just be himself for the first time ever. A knock on the interior door down to the garage interrupted his contemplation of the tilework.

"Hey, Lee! You in there?"

Lee strode over to the door and pulled it open. "Hey, boss. Come on in. What's up?"

Kirk's low whistle as they walked to the kitchen made him smile. "Wow! This looks amazing. I can't believe you've accomplished so much so quickly."

"Glad you like it. You paid for it."

"Again, *wow*. What a difference. I love it. The white cabinets with the granite countertops look fantastic together. The gray subway tiles and stainless appliances are so much better than rooster and avocado. What's left to do?"

"Just need to grout now. The backsplash was the last project. Go take a look at the rest, if you want."

Lee was happy to hear Kirk's comments of appreciation as he went through the completed space. "It looks wonderful. And that's the last project?"

"Yep."

"Great," Kirk exclaimed clapping his hands together. "Then you don't have an excuse not to come to my Labor Day weekend barbecue on Sunday." Kirk raised his hand to stop Lee's protest. "I know you're shy, but the guys from the garage will be there. It will be good for you to get out of this apartment and garage and interact with people. I'm not taking no for an answer."

"But..."

"No buts. You'll come or I'll track you down and drag you, kicking and screaming. Understood?"

Lee fought with himself a moment before realizing this wasn't a battle he could win. Kirk could out-stubborn a donkey once he got that look in his eyes. "Yes, sir," Lee answered with a sigh. "What do you want me to bring?"

* * * *

The weather the day of the party was absolutely perfect. The street was lined with the cars of other guests. *So much for hoping this wouldn't be a huge deal.* There were a lot of vehicles. Lee sat in his car breathing deeply, trying to stop his imminent panic attack. *You can do this. Go in, say hi, get some food then you can leave. You've got friends here. There has to be a corner.* After the pep talk, Lee stepped out of the car and made his way to the door. A sign hung there saying to just go around back.

Heading to the backyard, Lee was horrified to discover the entire space filled with people. He ducked through the back door to find where to leave the potato salad he'd been instructed to bring. Thankfully, it wasn't as crowded in there. He was able to drop it off on the counter and not have to talk to anyone. Glancing into the living room, he saw two little girls coloring at the coffee table.

"I can't do this right. It looks stupid," the little blonde girl whined.

"Yeah, that's not good," the little brunette agreed, right before noticing Lee standing there. "Oh hi. I'm Claire. I don't know you."

"I'm Lee. I work with Kirk."

"My Uncle Kirk talks about you," the little blonde answered. "I'm Sam."

"Hi, Sam. Hi, Claire. Nice to meet you. What do you have going on here?"

"I'm trying to draw a unicorn to give to our friend Lisa for her birthday. She likes unicorns, but my drawing looks stupid."

"Well, let me see. Maybe I can help." Lee made his way to the coffee table and knelt next to Sam. Picking up the drawing, he eyed it critically. "That's really not bad. I'm sure your friend will like it."

Looking at the dejection on the little girl's face, Lee felt the need to make it better. "Here... Give me a new piece of paper and let's see what I can do. Maybe if I draw it, you can color it. That way it's still from you. Would that work?"

"Can you draw?" Claire asked as she came to kneel on the other side of him.

"A little bit." Lee smirked before picking up a pencil and getting started. Five minutes later he put it down and noticed the girls staring at him in awe.

"Is it okay?"

"It's perfect," Sam breathed.

"Can you draw me a dragon?" Claire asked at the same time.

"Sure." Grabbing another piece of paper Lee started work on a dragon. *Now this is a great way to spend a party.*

"Ahem." A throat-clearing from the hall had all three of them jerking their heads up. The table was now filled with different drawings. The unicorn and dragon ones had somehow morphed into drawing an entire kingdom filled with castles and knights and princesses. The girls had definite opinions on what made a princess. She had to have a crown—but no frilly dresses. Dresses were stupid. She couldn't ride horses or fight bad guys in dresses.

"Hi, Daddy." Claire's deafening yell next to his ear had him flinching. "Look what Lee drew for us. It's a dragon and his name is Fred."

"Fred the dragon, huh?" Claire's dad was obviously amused as he took the drawing from Claire and glanced down at it. He started to look up to say something else, but his attention returned to the drawing for a longer look. "Wow. This *is* impressive."

Lee stood and shoved his hands in his pockets. "Thanks. Just fooling around."

"Oh, wait a minute. You're Lee? Good thing you're here. Kirk's been looking for you and was just starting to make noises about going to get you. Food's almost ready. Come on, girls. Lisa's here."

"Yay! Now I can give her the unicorn picture." Sam searched through the pile and snatched up the picture that had started the whole thing.

The man standing in the doorway held out his hand. "Eric Hallahan. I'm Claire's dad and Kirk's boyfriend. He's talked about you."

"Kirk's boyfriend?" Lee stepped closer and took the offered hand.

"Yep. Been together about a year and a half now." Eric's happiness with that fact was almost palpable. "I'm sorry your family was so ugly to you, but Kirk is very thankful to have you onboard. Said you worked miracles in that apartment and that your skills as a mechanic are very impressive."

"Yeah, I'm glad to be done with all the renovations. Between work and the apartment projects, I haven't had much chance to relax. It's nice to finally be done."

"Understandable. Well, come on. Let's go get some food.

Lee stepped out of the house onto the deck to find even more people in the backyard. There was a line forming around the tables of food. He was impressed with the sheer quantities. The tables were full. Lee joined the line and filled his plate before looking around for someone he knew to sit with. Spotting Will at a table in the corner, Lee made his way over.

"Hey, Will. Mind if I sit with you?"

"Not at all, my boy. Grab a spot. Hadn't seen you here."

"I was inside with the girls." Lee raised one shoulder in a half-shrug. "Much quieter in there."

"Yeah. Kirk and Eric's parties tend to be a bit crowded."

Lee snorted a laugh. "A bit? You could've warned me."

"Now where's the fun in that?" Will tried unsuccessfully to hide his smirk.

"Glad you think you're funny. So, Eric introduced himself as Kirk's boyfriend. I didn't realize he was gay."

"He doesn't hide it. Why am I not surprised you didn't pick up on it? One of these days you're going to have to lift your head up and pay attention to the rest of the world. You don't have to keep your head down so much anymore. No one here is going to judge."

Lee looked up into Will's firm stare. "I know. It's just tough for me."

"I know your dad was super hard on ya. It killed me to watch him and your brother tear you down all the time. You deserved better than that."

"Thanks, Will." Lee stared at the food on his plate as his cheeks heated.

"Eat. You don't eat enough to keep a bird alive."

"Actually, birds eat like half their weight in food a day. If I ate like that, I would probably be the size of a house."

"Nope. You would stress it all off, smartass. *Eat.*"

"I'm eating. I'm eating." Lee froze with a forkful of potato salad halfway to his lips. His mouth was still open as his attention was caught by the most beautiful man he'd ever seen and had never thought to see in person. He snapped it closed when Will poked him in the side.

"You okay there?"

Lee couldn't tear his gaze away from what surely must be an illusion of some kind on the other side of the yard. "Is that Saul Valencia, former NFL linebacker for the Raleigh Raptors?"

"Oh yeah. He's real tight with Eric. I guess they were teammates and roommates in college. After Eric blew out his knee for the second time, he decided he would prefer to walk later in life than continue to play football. They stayed roommates, though. Saul and Eric are partners in V & H Sports, the sporting goods store Eric started after college. Saul used to work with Eric in the off season but is taking a more active role now that he has retired.

"He's slimmed down."

Will scoffed. "Yeah. He's still a damn big boy, though." A sly look came into his eyes. "Hey, didn't you used to have his posters plastered all over your walls? Want me to introduce you?"

"Uh...no. I'm good." Lee went back to eating, keeping his eyes firmly fixed on his plate. *Okay.* Maybe he snuck a look or two at his fantasy man, but no way in hell was he going to talk to him. He would be devastated if the man turned out to be a douche. It was better to keep him as a fantasy.

"Hey, Eric, who's the redhead sitting over by Will? Haven't seen him here before," Saul asked.

"That's Kirk's newest mechanic...Lee. You've heard me talking about him. He's the one brave or stupid enough to tackle the eyesore apartment above the garage."

"Oh, man. You still owe me for helping clear out that mess. I've been in college frat houses cleaner than that."

"Well, according to Kirk, you could eat off the floors there now."

"That's good to know. Please tell me that hideous bathroom is gone."

"First thing Lee did."

"Uncle Saul! Uncle Saul!" A pint-sized dynamo came tearing across the yard and launched herself at him. He bent to scoop her up and give her a hug.

"Hi there, Claire-bear." A crinkling paper drew his attention. "Hey, what's this?"

"Lee drew me a dragon. Isn't he cool?"

Saul looked at the paper Claire held up for him. "Oh, wow. That's amazing."

"Yep. I told him about my dragon and he drew it."

"You are one lucky girl."

Another little voice cut in. "Hi, Uncle Saul."

Sam stood looking at him with big eyes. Even after more than a year, she still wasn't quite sure about him. He knelt to get eye level with her. "Hey there, Sam. Whatchya got there?"

"Lee drew a princess-knight picture for me. See?" After thrusting the picture into Saul's hand, she came around and placed her hand on his arm and started pointing at things in the picture. "It's me as a princess-knight and this is my trusty steed Doc."

"Doc?"

"Yep. Doc the horse."

"I like your purple armor."

"Yep. It's awesome." She whispered the words. "We're on a quest to slay Fred the dragon."

"Fred?"

"You'll never catch Fred. Fred's unstoppable." Then Claire made her dragon picture do a swooping attack of the princess-knight in purple armor before making it fly away. Sam took off after Claire, waving her own paper in the air.

"Fred the dragon?" Saul asked Eric.

"No idea where that came from. It's just what she named him."

"And Doc the horse?"

"Kirk says Sam has always insisted from the time she was little that every horse's name is Doc. It's a thing."

Saul laughed until he had to wipe the tears from his eyes. "Oh man, that's perfect."

"Did you catch how good those drawings were?"

"Oh yeah. The kid's got talent."

"Do you think he could —" Whatever he was going to ask was interrupted by Kirk's shrill whistle.

"Now that I have everyone's attention. Eric? Could you come over here, please?"

Saul was surprised to see that the usually unflappable Kirk had sweat dripping down his face and his hand was shaking a little bit when he raised it to beckon Eric closer. Saul exchanged a confused look with Eric before shrugging and giving Eric a shove in Kirk's direction.

Once Eric had reached Kirk, Kirk grabbed his hand. "Eric, I wanted to say in front of our friends and family here today that I love you. In fact, I am more in love with you every single day…even when you leave your dirty socks on the floor."

The last point garnered a bunch of chuckles throughout the crowd as everyone was aware what a neat freak Kirk was.

"I love you too, babe. You know that."

"I do know that, which is why…" Kirk dropped to one knee and pulled a ring box out of his pocket. "I was wondering if you would make it official and agree to marry me?"

Saul chuckled at Eric's wide-eyed look of shock then watched as tears filled his eyes before dripping onto his face.

"Baby? You're scaring me," Kirk said.

"What? Yes! Of course yes, you idiot." Reaching down, Eric yanked Kirk to his feet and engulfed him in his arms in a tight hug before pulling back and kissing him fiercely.

Saul felt a pang of envy pierce his heart. He would be ecstatic if he could find someone to adore him as much as these two men loved each other. For some reason, he turned to the gorgeous redhead to check his reaction to the scene. He was awestruck by the look of complete wonder and strong emotion on the face of the younger man. He must have sensed someone watching him, because his gaze raised to meet Saul's. Saul watched as he became wary then dropped his gaze to the plate of food in front of him.

Saul felt a zap of electricity in that one moment of direct eye contact. There was a connection there and Saul's soul settled, just like that. He'd never really believed in love at first sight, but he was damn sure he was going to get to know the redhead better. He saw Lee peek up at him from under his fall of bangs before a blush covered his face. *Oh yeah*. He was definitely going to have to figure out how to meet him.

Saul made his way over to extend his congratulations to his friends. Both Claire and Sam were screeching and jumping up and down in excitement. *Who knew that Kirk coming to take custody of his niece after his sister's death would lead to this moment?*

"Congratulations, Eric, Kirk. I'm so happy for you both."

"Phew. I'm just glad he said yes. I was going to wait until after the cake, but my nerves couldn't take it anymore. I think I lost five pounds in flop sweat."

Saul laughed before handing him the napkin he'd snagged on his way by the table. "Yeah, you look it too, dude. Here."

Saul pulled Eric into a hug. "Glad to see you truly happy again, my friend. It looks good on you."

"It feels good on me too." Eric clapped his hand on Saul's back as they pulled away from each other. "You do know this means you have to do the best man thing again, right?"

"Oh no, not the monkey suit. Can't I just pay for you guys to elope instead?" He took their laughter to mean that wasn't going to happen. "Seriously, man, I'd be honored to do the best man duties."

After speaking with them for a few more minutes, Saul glanced toward where Lee had been. He was surprised to find the table empty. Searching the space, he located Lee making his way around the side of the house. Will walking up prevented him from following, as he wanted.

"Hey, Saul… Good to see you, man." Will extended his hand to shake. "Congratulations, you two. Lee wanted me to tell you congratulations from him too. He had to go."

"Everything okay?" Kirk watched as Lee made his escape.

"It's all good. You know how shy he is. This was a lot." Will stopped to chuckle. "Plus, seeing his big crush here didn't help."

"His big crush?" Just that fast, Saul's attention was focused on Will.

"He had your posters all over his room growing up. His father used to go on and on about his weird fixation with you. That was before he found out the boy was gay. I'm sure he's figured out the whys of it now." Will fixed Saul with a hard stare. It didn't seem to matter to him that Saul had easily ten inches on the man and a hundred pounds. "I saw you looking at him. If you're really interested, I won't stand in your way, but don't bother if you're just looking to fool around. That boy has had enough bad in his life."

"What do you mean?"

"That's not my story to tell. Just go slow. As I said, he's shy. You're going to have to woo him if you want something real."

Eric chuckled. "Saul doesn't know the meaning of the word 'slow'. Freight train? Yes. Slow? Not so much."

"Well, if he's interested, he is going to have to learn," Will responded.

Will snapping at him was a surprise. The man was usually so laid-back. Saul made sure to maintain eye contact as he answered him. "I will."

Will studied him, obviously judging his sincerity before giving him a nod. "Alrighty then. Here's what you should do. You need to find a way to ask for his help. He's a sucker for that."

"I have just the thing too," Eric chimed in, "as I started to say earlier, after I saw how well he can draw."

"What do you mean?" Kirk asked. "What did he draw?"

Claire answered from where she was standing next to him. "He drew me a dragon. See?"

"And he drew me as a princess-knight. See?" Sam shoved her picture in front of Kirk's face too. Kirk took the pictures from the girls.

"Oh, wow. He said he drew as a hobby, but I had no idea he was this talented."

"What's your idea, Eric?" Saul asked.

"Well, I was thinking we could get him to work on a mural for the wall at the back of the flagship store. As an added bonus, it would give you an excuse to talk to him."

"Yeah. Giving Lee a subject to discuss is important. Add in a project where he feels like he's helping and it's a great way for you to get to know him." Will fixed Saul with another pointed stare. "If you hurt the boy, though, I will come looking for you. Understood?"

"Yep. Got it." Saul smiled, but he wouldn't discount the seriousness of Will's intent.

Chapter Two

Saul shuffled his feet. Waiting was *so* not his strong suit. He was holding bags of leftovers from yesterday's barbecue. They had decided to bring Lee lunch and talk to him about what they needed from him. The girls had insisted on coming to see their new best friend too, so it was a bit more crowded for this visit than he'd thought it would be.

"Knock again."

"The place isn't that big, Saul," Kirk said.

"His truck's here. The fence was locked. He has to be here. Try calling him."

Kirk shook his head but did as asked, pulling out his phone and dialing. Saul tilted his head, listening to the sound of the Mr. Clean jingle coming from somewhere above them.

"Is that Lee's ringtone for you?" Saul couldn't help but chuckle. "It fits."

Kirk tried to look stern but Saul could tell he was amused too. Kirk turned toward the ladder leading to the roof to the right of the doorway. "Come on. Let's go make sure he's okay. He isn't answering his phone either." Sam went next with Eric behind her.

Looping the bag handles over his arms, Saul followed last, making sure Claire climbed safely. He needn't have worried. She climbed the ladder like a monkey, without a moment's hesitation.

Glancing around, he didn't see Lee immediately. Saul's attention was snagged by movement in the greenhouse when Lee suddenly straightened from where he'd been slouched in front of a canvas. Lee winced then raised his hand to rub the muscles in the left side of his neck. He must have fallen asleep with his head against the glass wall beside him — not the most comfortable way to rest.

"Hey, Lee." Kirk made his way across the roof, stopping when he reached the door.

The girls scooted past him and right over to Lee.

"You okay?" Kirk asked.

"Hey —" Lee's voice was a raspy mess. He cleared his throat and tried again. "Hello. What time is it?"

Lee looked around then down at himself. His befuddlement was adorable. He was covered in a rainbow of paints with a paintbrush stuck behind his ear and several others laid out around him. Lee reached for a rag and started wiping his hands off. There was another jolt of awareness when Lee made accidental eye contact with Saul, but Lee's gaze moved on to Kirk and Eric. Seeing them must have reminded him of what he'd been working on because he attempted to block their view of his canvas.

"Oh, wow. You've done all that since yesterday?" Kirk asked with awe in his voice.

"That's us!" Claire squealed.

Saul took a closer look at the canvas. It was a painting of Kirk proposing to Eric. Lee had painted both girls standing behind them, clapping. The pure emotion of the moment came shining through—the sweat on Kirk's brow, the tears of happiness in Eric's eyes, the smiles on the girls' faces…but mostly the love. The picture glowed with it. Lee had obviously fallen asleep while working on the background, but the main part of the painting was complete.

Lee must have become aware of the silence around him. Looking up, he found everyone staring at him. "It was supposed to be a surprise. I was going to give it to you as an engagement present." He spoke so fast that the words all tumbled over themselves. "I guess I should've gotten permission first. I'm sorry."

Kirk yanked him into a hug. "What? No! It's fantastic. *Never* apologize for doing something so nice. Wow, dude, you humble me with your talent. It will get pride of place at our house. Seriously. That's amazing."

Eric grabbed Lee next and gave him a hug too. "It's perfect. Thank you so much."

Lee slumped back onto his stool as soon as Eric let him go, busying himself with straightening his supplies. "Well, I need to finish it and it will need to dry before you take it anywhere." Reaching up, he switched off the light behind him. Then a look of pure panic crossed Lee's face before he darted for the doorway.

"Excuse me. Be right back."

"Where are you going?"

"Need to make sure I didn't leave anything on the stove."

"What?" Kirk chuckled behind him.

They all followed Lee down the stairs and toward the kitchen. Lee gave long huff of breath then relaxed.

"What was that all about?" Kirk came to stand next to Saul and peeked into the kitchen. "There's nothing on the stove."

A wave of red rose up Lee's face and into his hairline. With a chuckle, Saul wondered how low the color went.

"I tend to zone out when I'm working. I didn't remember turning on the light in the greenhouse, so I needed to make sure I didn't come grab something to eat at some point." A loud grumble came from the vicinity of his stomach.

"I would say your stomach is answering that one for you," Kirk said.

"You could hear that?"

"Heck, I'm standing over here and I could hear it," Saul teased from his place at the bottom of the stairs. His attention was caught by the stunning bathroom to his right. "Wow. What an improvement. I'm impressed."

Eric whistled as he came up beside Kirk. "Come see the miracles he worked in the kitchen."

Saul pretended to look at the kitchen while keeping an eye on Lee. He didn't like how the man's eyes darted around, as if looking for an escape route.

"Excuse me," Lee mumbled as he ducked under Eric's arm and made his way to the other side of the living space. "What are you all doing here anyway?"

Saul raised one of the bags of food he had in his hands. "We brought lunch. I'm Saul, by the way. We never got a chance to meet yesterday."

"Um…Lee." Lee hesitated a moment then reached out and offered a handshake.

Saul switched both bags to one hand and gladly accepted, not really surprised to feel a jolt of connective electricity when their hands touched. It had obviously surprised Lee, though, if his rapid pulling back of his hand was any indication. Lee wiped his hands on his pants legs.

"Nice to meet you. Why did you bring lunch again?" The look of confusion was absolutely adorable, but wisely Saul kept that observation to himself. He didn't think Lee would be very receptive to comments like that.

"Well, because we wanted to, and we have a business proposition for you."

Lee's eyes instantly went wary. "What kind of business proposition?" Lee's stomach grumbled even more angrily.

"First, let's feed you, then we'll talk about it."

"Um… Can you give me ten minutes to shower? I feel absolutely grungy."

"Sure. Take your time. We'll set up lunch on the roof."

The group made their way back upstairs. It truly was the only area that had enough seating for all of them. Ten minutes later Lee joined them. His hair was still dripping a little but was combed and he had on clean clothes.

"Great! You made it. Grab a plate and take what you want."

Lee served himself and they all dug in to the food. As it was devoured, there wasn't much conversation. Saul looked up to see Kirk staring at Lee with openmouthed amazement.

"Geez, Lee, when was the last time you ate?" Kirk asked. "I haven't even eaten half my sandwich yet."

"Um… Yesterday at your party?"

"That was almost twenty-four hours ago." Kirk's disapproving tone had Lee dropping his head and blushing again.

"Sorry. The muse just takes over, ya know?"

"I can't really say I understand, not having one of those, but slow down a bit or you're going to be sick."

"Yes, Dad."

Saul chuckled. "Wow, I don't think you could have put more sarcasm in that comment if you tried. I'm impressed. I didn't think you had it in you."

Lee shared a brief look and a smirk, before returning his attention to his food. Saul did a mental fist pump at the first sign of Lee starting to relax in his presence. Finally, everyone had eaten enough and they sat back with their drinks. The girls were playing with the dolls they had brought with them. From what Saul could see and hear, Claire's Barbie was the drill sergeant making the G.I. Joe dolls do pushups and other exercises.

"So, what's going on?" Lee asked after a few moments of silence.

"You missed a lot by leaving early yesterday," Kirk answered.

"I did?"

"Yep. Personal first. After you left, we were all talking about how Eric and I needed to find a bigger house that would fit all of us comfortably, but we really didn't want to leave the neighborhood. It seems that the Andersons down the street are wanting to downsize, but they really didn't want to leave the neighborhood either."

"And the Andersons have a pool!" Claire added from her place on the ground.

Eric chuckled. "And the Andersons have a pool. So, what's going to happen is this… Kirk and I are going to buy their house. The Andersons are going to buy Kirk's house and we'll put my house on the market after we do the few updates we want to do on their house before we move in."

Kirk took over the explanation. "Win-win for everyone. That's where *you* come in."

"I do? How?"

Kirk reached over and slapped Lee on the back. "The girls have requested a mural in their playroom, painted by you. They'd like you to paint their kingdom that you all created onto their wall."

Sam crawled over and put her hand on Lee's knee, looking up at him beseechingly. "Please, Lee. Please say you'll do it."

Claire crawled over and put her hand on Lee's other knee. "Yeah, Lee. Please?"

"We'll pay you for your time, of course." Eric jumped in.

"Pleeeeeassssee?" The girls begged in unison. The puppy eyes really weren't fair.

Saul saw the exact moment Lee caved even before he opened his mouth to answer them. "Okay, I'll do it. I have work, though, so it'll probably be slow."

"Yay! Yay!" The girls jumped up and screamed their joy.

"All right. All right." Kirk reached out and grabbed Sam in a hug while Eric did the same to Claire. "Go back to your playing. We need to discuss the other bit with Lee now."

"You mean there's *more*?" Lee's eyes went huge in shock.

"Yep-p." Saul dragged out the word making sure to make the 'p' pop. Once he had Lee's attention, he continued, "We need help with another mural. We'd like one for the back wall of our flagship store. What do you think? Does it sound like something you could do for us?"

"You do know I'm not a professional, right? I just paint for fun and a few times I did some paintwork on a few projects at my dad's shop. I've taken a few classes at the community college, but I'm nowhere near a pro. A lot of people are going to see the mural at the store. Are you sure you want me to do it? I usually draw on a smaller scale — and not someone else's ideas."

"Well, all we're asking is for you to try. From what we've seen, we think you could do a great job on it. We know you're already pretty busy with work. Kirk has agreed to let us borrow you tomorrow afternoon to give you a tour of our offices and the flagship store. That'll give you a better idea of what we're about. We will, of course, pay you for your time for this as well."

Lee looked to Kirk. "If you're sure you don't mind?"

"Not at all. I think it'll be a good thing for all of you. We can certainly do without you for one afternoon. We don't have a whole lot on the books, it being the day after the holiday and all."

Lee sat deep in thought for a minute before raising his head and looking at Eric. "I'll do it. It sounds interesting."

"Great. Then we'll get out of your hair and let you enjoy the rest of your long weekend. Come on, girls. Collect your stuff and let's go."

"Aw, Dad. We haven't had a chance to talk to Lee about our picture yet."

Lee chuckled. "I think I have a pretty good idea from before. How about I draw some things up and we can meet some other time to see if you approve."

Sam's eyes lit up. "You mean like a business meeting? Eric has lots of those."

"Yeah. We can call it that if you want."

"Yay! We get to have a business meeting, Claire."

"Yes!" Taking on a more sophisticated tone, Claire looked at Lee, waved her hand and said, "Please have your people call my people and we'll set up a time." The girls then looked at each other and dissolved into giggles.

"All right, you two lunatics, let's go." Kirk muttered under his breath to Eric, "'Have your people call my people.' Where do they come up with this stuff?"

Eric pulled Kirk to him for a brief peck on the lips. "No idea, but life would certainly be boring without them."

"That's certainly true."

The girls headed to the ladder. "Um, girls, you can go through my apartment and down the regular stairs. You don't have to use the ladder."

"Aw. Where's the fun in that?" Claire whined.

"Girls. Stairs. Now," Eric ordered.

Saul had to cover his laugh with a cough when Claire huffed her way to the stairs. Then he turned and spoke to Eric. "Oh, man, when Claire becomes a true teen, you guys are going to have your hands full."

"Don't I know it. At least Sam will be there too, to hopefully talk her out of her crazier ideas." Eric sighed as he finished picking up the last of the mess before heading to the stairs to follow the girls.

"They're both great," Lee said, then seemed surprised he'd said anything. "Sorry. It's just…"

"No. We know," Kirk told him, clasping his shoulder before he, too, headed for the stairs. "We're lucky. They're good kids."

"And you have each other," Saul added. Kirk shot them a brilliant smile over his shoulder, the adoration for his fiancé a tangible thing.

Saul looked to Lee, but wasn't sure what he saw there. *Envy? Loneliness? Well, I can certainly relate to both of those things.* He waited until Kirk went through the doorway to speak to Lee.

"Lee?" Lee jumped. "You know if my ego wasn't strong, I would feel bad that you forgot I was here."

"I could never forget you were here." Lee's eyes went wide as he realized what he'd just said. "No. I mean..." Lee closed his eyes and dropped his head.

"Flustered is a good look on you." Saul took a step closer and raised his hand to the side of Lee's neck. Lee leaned into the touch for just a moment before pulling away.

"Glad you like it. You'll probably see it a lot."

"Nah. You'll get used to me."

"I will?" Lee snapped his head up and he looked at Saul.

"Yep. You're going to get used to me then you're going to reach a point where you can't remember a time when I wasn't there."

"What?"

"Everyone has told me to take it slow with you and I will. But slow doesn't mean that I'm not going to make my intentions clear. We have a connection. I know you feel it too. I'd like to see where it'll take us."

"You do? Meaning what exactly?" Lee licked his lips as he waited for Saul's answer.

"Dating. You, me, dinner."

"You want to take me out on a date? *Me*?" Lee pointed at himself.

Saul couldn't help but chuckle as he stepped close and again raised his hand to the side of Lee's neck. "Do you see anyone else here?"

"Um…no, but why would you want to date *me*? I'm nobody. I'm just a mechanic."

"You are not 'just' anything. I barely know you, but everything I've seen about you so far says you're amazing."

Lee searched his eyes. Saul guessed he was judging his sincerity. He must have realized Saul meant what he said because the blush deepened and Lee tried to pull away.

"No way." Saul wrapped his other arm around Lee and pulled him closer, moving his hand from the side of his neck to the back of his head. "I'm serious. I think you're amazing and one day you'll think so too. For some reason, you seem blind to how wonderful you are. We're going to work on changing that."

"Why me? You could have anyone you want. I mean you're Saul Valencia. *The* Saul Valencia — capital letters, copyright and all."

Saul chuckled at that description. "Capital letters? Really?" He sobered. "I'm just a man, Lee. Yes, I was a good football player. Yes, I made a lot of money doing it. But — and this is a big 'but' — I had to hide who I really was the whole time. I couldn't be gay and play the game I loved. I couldn't go out on dates with men who interested me. Everything was all about sneaking around. I don't want to be Saul Valencia 'all in caps' anymore.

"I don't need to be 'something for everybody'. I want to be 'Saul who is everything to one somebody'. I need you to think about it. We have the meeting tomorrow. I would very much like it if you went out to dinner with me after the meeting. Just to be clear…on a date, not a continuation of our business meeting. You think about it and let me know if you think you would be willing to give this thing between us a chance."

Saul couldn't resist the temptation anymore and pressed his lips to Lee's. His intention had been to keep it light, but one taste and he wanted more. He used the hand on the back of Lee's head to press him closer, pushing his tongue between Lee's lips. Lee opened easily for him and he pushed his tongue out shyly to press against Saul's. Saul groaned his pleasure.

"Hey, Saul, you coming?"

Kirk's voice echoing up the stairwell made Saul remember where he was. He pressed another brief kiss to Lee's lips before reluctantly releasing him and stepping back. He cleared his throat before yelling back to Kirk. "Yeah, be down in a minute." Quieter, he spoke only to Lee. "I really didn't mean to get carried away there. Think about what I said and let me know when I see you tomorrow." He ran his finger down Lee's jaw. "I really think we could have something great."

Saul spun on his heel and forced himself to move to the stairs. It ranked up there as one of the hardest things he'd ever done. Caveman instinct wanted him to drag Lee off to his lair and lay claim. *Slow*. Everyone said slow. *Ugh*.

"Saul?" Lee's voice stopped him, and he swung his head around to look at him.

"Yes, Lee."

"I'll see you tomorrow for the meeting" — Lee paused to take a deep breath before continuing — "and our date."

Saul's grin was so big it hurt his face. "Yeah?"

"Yeah, let's give this a shot."

Saul strode back across the roof to give Lee a quick peck. "You won't regret it."

"I just hope *you* won't. Let me walk you down."

Chapter Three

"Hey, Lee, what're you still doing here? I thought you had to leave for your meeting ten minutes ago." Kirk's yell echoed through the apartment from his position standing outside his screen door.

"Kirk" — Lee walked from his bedroom wearing jeans and carrying the two shirts he had finally narrowed down to choose from for wearing to the meeting and dinner — "thank God you're here. Help!"

Kirk pulled open the door and made his way inside. "What's going on?"

"I don't know what to put on. What do people wear on dates?"

"First, take a deep breath. It'll be okay."

"I see you trying to hide your smile. This isn't funny!" Lee shook the shirt in his left hand in Kirk's direction.

Kirk didn't even bother hiding his laugh this time. "It kinda is. Relax! You already know he's interested. You just need to be yourself. Now what would you be most comfortable in?"

"Sweatpants and a T-shirt," Lee grumbled. He knew he was pouting but he just didn't care. "This is why I don't date. It's too much work."

"You haven't dated until now because you were still living at home with a homophobic father and brother. It has nothing to do with it being too much work. Chill out. Pick the green striped dress shirt. It will bring out the color of your eyes."

"Yeah?" Lee put on the shirt and tucked it in as he did up his belt. "I just don't understand why he's even interested. I'm boring. I don't know how to flirt. I'm hopeless."

Kirk grabbed him by both of his shoulders and gave him a little shake, forcing Lee to look at him. "You're a great mechanic, a great artist and a wonderful person. Anyone would be lucky to date you." Kirk accompanied the word lucky with another firm shake. "Saul is a great guy or I wouldn't let him anywhere near you. Trust me and Will, if you don't trust yourself to know you and Saul could be good for each other."

"But why me? I don't see where I could possibly offer him anything he doesn't already have."

"Is that what you're worried about?"

Lee nodded. "He's already amazing. He knows who he is and where he's going. I'm still trying to figure all that out."

"You're more together than you give yourself credit for. You're an amazing artist, which I'm sure your father didn't approve of." Kirk raised an eyebrow in inquiry.

Lee winced. "No. He thought it was girly and wanted me to not waste my time. The only positive he saw in the art was the special projects he booked in, where I got to do custom artwork on some cars and a motorcycle once."

"But you didn't stop drawing, and when it became unbearable to be around the hate, you moved out. You're creating a life for yourself, one step at a time. That's how you need to approach this thing with Saul as well. One step at a time. He's not going to propose marriage today. It's a first date. Go. Ask questions. Answer questions. Be the amazing person you already are."

"You make it sound so simple."

"The process *is* simple. It's the individuals involved that make it either difficult or easy. Both people have to put in the work and be honest about what they need and are looking for. Can you do that?"

"I can try. It's not really my normal mode. I'm used to doing what I need to do to keep the peace."

"That's not going to make you happy in a relationship in the long run. That's one of the reasons I think you and Saul will be a good match. He won't let you hide. He needs… Never mind. You have to figure it out with him. Give it a shot, okay?"

Lee nodded and took a deep breath, letting it out slowly.

Kirk stepped back and clapped his hands. "Now, you have to go or you're going to be late for your meeting. You've got this."

Lee nodded again before turning to pick up his wallet and keys from the basket on the table and his notebook and pen for writing down details from where he'd set them by the door. He double-checked that the envelope for the girls was still tucked into the notebook before following Kirk out of the door. He locked up and, with a wave for Kirk, made his way to his truck. The drive to Eric's office was short — too short for Lee to have time for another panic attack.

He gave himself a mental pep talk as he put the truck in Park, then gripped the steering wheel tightly to try to channel his nerves. "You've got this. One step at a time. Are you a man or a mouse?"

Lee would forever deny the squeak that came out of his mouth in response to the knock on his window. Whipping his head around, he jolted to find both Eric and Saul standing outside his window. Lee reached over and opened the door a little, waiting for the two men to step back before he opened the door the rest of the way and climbed out.

Lee took the offered handshake from Eric, "Sorry, Lee. I didn't mean to startle you. We were just coming back from lunch and saw you park."

He stuck out his hand to Saul as well but felt himself blush when Saul used the grip of his hand to pull him in for a peck on the lips.

"Hi, babe."

"Um…hi. Let me just grab my notebook."

Turning to the truck, Lee almost brained himself on the still-open door behind him. *Dork,* Lee chastised himself before repositioning so he could safely get his notebook from the passenger seat. Lee heard a groan behind him and looked back to catch Saul staring at his ass. Lee flushed harder. Saul just grinned when he made eye contact. Lee shook his head and straightened.

"You don't have a shy bone in your body, do you?" he said to Saul.

"No. Being shy has never been a problem for me."

"What about with your crush in college?" Eric interjected.

"Yeah. Well, what happened to the pact never to speak of it? *Ever.*"

"You see, Lee—"

"Oh no. If anyone is going to tell him the story, it'll be me. I'll tell you over dinner. I don't need anyone overhearing my humiliation."

"Surely it wasn't that bad."

Eric busted out laughing. Hard. "Oh, it was. It was epic."

"Should you be giving him such a hard time about it if it was so painful? I thought you were his friend." As soon as he'd finished speaking, Lee raised a hand to his mouth. "I'm so sorry, Eric. I don't know where that came from."

Saul raised his hand to halt his apology. "It's okay, Lee. I like that you're protective of me. As far as Eric giving me a hard time? He has certainly earned the right as my best friend. I certainly never let him live down his past blunders."

"Isn't that the truth? Unfortunately for me, I had a lot more of them than this guy here. I'm a slow learner."

"Come on. Let's go on inside and get the tour of the store done, both inside and out. Then we can brainstorm some ideas. We need to be out of here by five-thirty so we can make our reservations for dinner."

"Reservations? I'm not really dressed for anywhere that requires reservations."

"You're fine. I'm going like this." Lee took in Saul's khakis and polo shirt with the store logo. His gaze got stuck on the man's broad chest stretching the material of the shirt. He yanked his head up at Saul's chuckle.

"Eyes are up here, gorgeous."

Lee groaned before turning to follow Eric. At this rate, his cheeks were going to stay some shade of purple. He just knew it.

He was still following Eric as they made their way from seeing the inside to a large grassy area outside between the store and another building. The way the store had been originally built, it made an L-shape in the back and connected to the building next door.

"This was your first store?"

"Yep, and we've kept the offices above it, even as we expanded. We've recently purchased this building next door. We're going to move the offices over there on the lower floors and Saul is having an apartment built upstairs for himself."

"Easy commute," Saul added. "I am *so* not a morning person and the location is great for walking to local restaurants and such."

"Words of advice. Don't try to talk to Saul before ten a.m. or at least two cups of coffee. He's a bit of a bear until then."

"Please tell me you aren't a morning person," Saul said to Lee.

Lee couldn't help his chuckle at Saul's pleading expression. "Nah. I'm more of a night owl, but I'm pretty even keel most of the time."

"Phew, good to hear. I don't need to cancel the reservation then."

Lee looked up to verify that Saul was indeed joking. "Wait... I thought I heard today that you were buying Eric's house?"

"I am, for my parents to use. It's going to be a surprise for them. I'm going to still live in the apartment. My mom likes to visit, and sometimes one or more of my sisters and their children come with her. This way, they have their own space, but Eric can keep an eye on the place when they aren't here. I can stay in my apartment and have my privacy."

"Oh yeah. That's a great idea. Save your sanity," Eric added.

"I know, right?"

"Why?" Lee was very confused.

"Saul has a big family — four sisters, all with at least two kids of their own. Saul's the youngest."

"It means I had four extra moms growing up. They all like to tell me what to do."

"Really? I can't picture that at all."

"You should see it. The four of them plus their mom simultaneously baby him, try to feed him and question all his life choices. His dad just sits back and lets them do it, too. It's hysterical to watch."

"You forgot 'interrogate me as to when I'm going to find a nice boy and settle down'."

"They know you're gay?"

"Oh yeah. It was necessary to tell them. They kept trying to set me up with all their girlfriends, although my sister Lucia knew. She caught me staring at some guy in some magazine of hers when I was twelve. She was the only one still living at home when I hit my teen years. She kept it quiet, though. She said it wasn't her secret to tell."

"Huh. That was nice of her. Are you closest to Lucia, then?"

"No, actually I'm closest to Lexie, my oldest sister. We're both here in the Raleigh area. The others all live in Florida. They come to visit a couple of times a year. My parents' visits have been getting longer and longer, though. They really like it here. What about you?"

"Uh, my mom died when I was fourteen. Breast cancer. It was just me, my dad and my older brother."

"Were you ever close to them?"

"Nah. My mom was the one I was close to. She kind of acted as the interpreter between me and my dad. Um, did there used to be another building here or something?"

Eric and Saul exchanged a look before they stepped up to scope out the grassy area with him. Thankfully, they went along with his subject change. He so didn't want to get into his messed-up family dynamics.

Saul answered, "As far as we can tell from records, the original owners had an area here for their children to play. They lived in the apartment above the store. It was a walled-off area for them. There used to be more grass and a couple of trees."

"What happened?"

"It seems a car crashed into the wall and destroyed it at about the same time he was ready to retire. By this point, the kids were off to college or had settled elsewhere. The owner had the debris removed and left it, rather than spend more money to replace it."

"That's too bad. I'm sure it was really lovely at one point."

Eric clapped his hands and joined the conversation. "Yes, and I'm looking for ideas of what you think we could do with the space. I mean, we could set up some space for people to test our products. What do you think?"

"I think that's a way for you to lose product."

"True," Eric conceded with a sigh. "Well, I do want to have trees and benches put in this one corner to make a place for people to come to relax. It would be good if we could have the V & H Sporting Goods logo painted on the wall over there. Do you think that's something you could do as well?"

"Honestly, I'm a little concerned that, if you leave it open like this, it will become a place for graffiti artists. Do your employees have a space to relax and eat their lunch?"

"Wow, look at him, watching out for everyone." Saul's putting his arm around Lee's shoulders made him jump. He hadn't realized Saul was standing that close.

"Easy there. I didn't mean to startle you."

"It's okay. I wasn't expecting you to touch me is all." Lee scooted out from under his arm and walked deeper into the area. "Do we have measurements on the walls?"

"Yep. I have them up in the office. Come on. Let's get out of the heat and grab something to drink." Eric turned and headed to the front door.

"I can't believe it's still this hot in September." Saul groaned, snagging Lee's hand to pull him along as he turned to follow Eric.

Lee stared at their laced fingers a moment before focusing on the conversation again. "How long have you lived here? It's always still hot in September. At least this year you don't have to practice in it."

"I've lived here since college, so that's… What? About thirteen years? I'm certainly *not* missing pre-season workouts or games. Those were brutal in this heat."

"I can imagine. I certainly didn't miss the training camps in this heat after my arm was busted up," Lee said.

"Wait! Did you used to play football?"

"Yeah, but then my arm was broken and I couldn't play anymore." Lee ended with a shrug.

"What position?"

"Quarterback."

"Were you any good?"

Lee shrugged again. "I guess I was decent." He'd been more than decent. That had been why… Lee stopped that train of thought before it could go any further. Saul was way too perceptive and he didn't need him asking questions. "But back to what we were talking about. We had all sorts of problems with dehydration during the camps for high school. Some kids died from it at some schools nearby."

"Yeah, I know. It's one of the training classes we want to offer coaches in the area, signs and treatment of dehydration. It's no joke."

"No, it really isn't. Is that part of the reason for the new office space?"

"Yep. We're setting aside a training room to offer different classes, from how to make sure the equipment fits right to techniques and some medical stuff. We have some EMTs and doctors signed on to do the medical classes—signs of concussion, signs of dehydration…stuff like that."

"Sounds like a great idea. I hope the coaches in the area will sign up."

"We've gotten a great response from people. The first class is scheduled for six weeks from now. There's already a waiting list."

"That's awesome."

"Since it was my idea, I'm glad you think so." Saul's deep chuckle made Lee shiver. He tried to hide it, but he didn't think he was totally successful, if Saul's self-satisfied look was any indication. Thankfully, they were interrupted by Eric coming into the room with three water bottles and a pad of paper. A rolled-up blueprint was tucked under his arm.

"Here we go, guys." Eric sat in the chair across from them after handing out the water bottles. After setting his own to the side, Eric rolled out the blueprint. "These are the specs the landscaping guy came up with for the outdoor space. As you can see, the corner here is going to have trees and benches for people to relax. Other than that, I'm open to ideas. The measurements of each of the walls are here too."

After he'd rolled the blueprint back up, he handed it to Lee.

"Are there more copies? I don't want to take your only one."

"Don't worry about it. I have extras. Now, any other questions?"

"I don't think so. I need time to process all this. I'll give some thought to what else could be done with the outdoor space and try to figure out something for the mural. Give me a week or so. Okay?"

"Of course, it's okay. There's no rush. This project isn't going anywhere. It's just an idea."

"Great. Which reminds me…" Lee reached into the notebook he'd placed on the table and pulled out the envelope he had stashed there. He handed the envelope to Eric. "This is for the girls to look at. I hope they like it."

"The envelope is sealed. Why is the envelope sealed?" The look of bewilderment on Eric's face amused Lee and he couldn't stop his chuckle.

"Because it's the girls' project and they should be the first ones to see it."

"He just met you and he already knows you," Saul said with a chuckle of his own. "Nosy busybodies…you and Kirk both."

"I am *so* not a nosy busybody. I am not denying Kirk is—"

"Not denying Kirk is what?"

Kirk's voice from the doorway made them all jump.

"A nosy busybody," Saul answered helpfully as Eric started to squirm.

"Oh, really? Pot, meet kettle," Kirk retorted.

"Which was exactly my point," Saul said.

"Anyway… Do you know what Lee did? He put the drawing for the girls' playroom in a sealed envelope, so the girls would be the first to see it," Eric explained.

"Okay and? That makes sense to me. It's their room."

"Really? You're going to take Lee's side on this?"

"The suspense is killing you, isn't it, babe?" Kirk pulled Eric into a hug and gave him a quick peck on the lips.

"It really is." Eric pouted.

Lee couldn't hold in the laughter anymore. Anyone over six foot should not pout. Eric's affronted look just made Lee laugh harder until his sides hurt.

Chapter Four

Lee tried to take a couple of hopefully unnoticeable calming breaths. In his wildest fantasies about him and Saul—and yes, he had to admit if only to himself that there were a lot of them—he'd never thought he would be sitting across a table from him. Ever. On a *date*. What the hell could they possibly have in common to talk about?

"So," Saul interrupted his downward-spiraling thoughts.

Lee looked up at Saul then quickly lowered his gaze to the menu in front of him. The steakhouse restaurant they were sitting in was way above the quality of the kind of place he could afford. *Heck, what is the cheapest thing on the menu?*

Saul took it out of Lee's hands. "Why don't you just let me order for you? I can see you panicking. Any allergies?"

Lee winced. "It's that obvious?"

"Yep."

"Sorry. No allergies. I'm just…"

"Nervous. I get it. I'm nervous too."

"You? Why would *you* be nervous?"

"Well, I hid being gay for a very long time. I didn't date, with one exception. I just hooked up. Quietly. I haven't exactly come out. I just stopped hiding that I'm gay. My friends know. My family knows. The public"—Saul waved around at the restaurant and the people sitting in it—"doesn't know and, really, it's none of their business—but someone could think it is. I really want a chance with you, though."

"I would like a chance with you too, but my family hates that I'm gay. I had to keep my friends quiet so they wouldn't draw my brother's attention. To be honest, I've been hiding at Kirk's garage. The restoration project was the excuse I needed to not go anywhere."

"Why are you hiding? You're safe with Kirk and his employees."

"I know that. It's just—" Lee was interrupted by the arrival of the waitress with the drinks they had ordered. A Coca-Cola for him and a beer for Saul. Saul gave him a look that said the conversation wasn't over, before turning to the waitress and placing their food order.

After the waitress had left, Saul pinned him with a hard stare. "I need you to explain. Why do you feel you need to hide?"

Lee ran his hand through his hair, wishing he hadn't opened his big mouth. "My home life wasn't like yours. My father and brother hate me, my father partly because I look like my mother and he says I remind him of her. My brother just hates me. He used any excuse growing up to make my life hell. You asked about me playing football." At Saul's nod he continued, "I was really good. Loved the game. Was following in my dad's and brother's footsteps being a quarterback for our high school team."

"Okay, so why was that a bad thing?"

"It wasn't, until I was getting ready to pass my brother's touchdown passing record after my sophomore year."

"Your brother didn't like it, I take it?"

"My brother broke my arm two days before football camp so I couldn't play my junior year." At Saul's look of horror, Lee forced himself to continue. "He told Dad it was an accident, that he'd tripped and accidentally knocked me down the stairs, but you should've seen the look on his face." Lee shuddered. "It was pure evil. It only got worse for me when he found out I was gay."

"How does it get worse than broken limbs?"

"He stopped pretending they were accidents."

"Oh, Lee" — Saul reached out and took Lee's hand — "nothing like that will happen to you at Kirk's. From what I've heard, everyone adores you and you have amazing skills as a mechanic."

"Well, that's mainly from Will. He kind of took me under his wing when he worked for my dad."

"I'm glad you had Will."

"Me too. He and my artwork are what got me through. My mistake was letting my dad and brother see what I could do."

"What do you mean?" Saul asked, rubbing his thumb against the back of Lee's hand, interrupting his train of thought.

Pulling his gaze away from the sight with effort, he continued his story.

"It's what led to them finding out I was gay. We had a client come into the shop who wanted a custom paint job on his Harley, not something my dad's shop typically did. I heard them talking, told my dad I could do it and showed the customer the sketch I'd made while he'd been describing what he wanted. The guy was thrilled. My dad was happy that he could make the money off the project. He gave me a whole hundred-dollar bonus on top of my hourly rate for the two-thousand-five-hundred-dollar project." Lee circled his finger in the air to indicate his sarcastic excitement with the bonus.

Saul barked out a laugh. "Big spender."

"I know...right?"

They paused when the waitress brought their salads and some bread for the table.

After she'd left, Saul prodded him to continue. "What happened next?"

"Like I said, the customer was thrilled. My brother was" — Lee paused and took a breath — "intrigued is the best word I can think of at the moment. It was like he was just waiting for that last detail to confirm something for him. The whole time I was doing the project, he made comments about how only a faggot would be that good and asking me if I was queer. Was I hoping the bike's owner would want to do me? Is that why I'd spoken up? After it was done and my dad was so happy with me, my brother stepped things up, started getting louder with his questions and got the other guys in the shop to start giving me a hard time. A couple of them went to my dad and said they weren't going to work with a queer."

Lee stopped to take a sip of his water. Looking up at Saul, he was astounded to see that Saul was visibly upset.

"What did your dad do? I'm guessing nothing good, since you now work for Kirk."

"No, nothing good. He came and asked me if it was true and I was just so tired of hiding, so tired of trying to pretend to be something I wasn't, of trying to make everyone happy but me."

"You told him the truth," Saul stated rather than asked.

"Yeah, I told him the truth. I thought my dad was going to have a heart attack. He turned this really bright shade of red then told me to clear out my stuff at work and at home and get out. My brother was just over his shoulder smirking at me, like he'd won some prize."

"What did you do?"

"I packed up my tools and loaded them into my truck then went home to pack up the rest of my stuff. What else was I going to do?"

"I don't know. Try to talk to your dad, maybe?"

"You don't know my dad. He'd made a decision. He considers it a weakness to change your mind on anything. Once a decision is made, that's it with him."

"Wow. That's a tough way to be."

"He says that's what it means to be a man."

"Okay. So, what happened after that? There must be more to the story. Eric said you showed up with bruises."

Lee sighed deeply. "Yeah, well, I wasn't fast enough at the house. I'd just put the final load into the truck when my brother and his buddies showed up to '*teach the fag a lesson*' — their words, not mine. I fought back, but it was four against one. I was lucky that our neighbor was a cop. He showed up and stopped them. He asked me if I wanted to press charges. I just wanted to be done, so I said 'no' and left. Does that make me weak?"

"No, that makes you human," Saul reassured him while taking his hand again.

"Yeah, well, Kirk's place has been amazing for me. Everyone is so friendly, and no one cares who has sex with who. I can actually sleep." Lee cut himself off, but it was too late. He saw Saul's eyes.

"What do you mean you can sleep? Was that not the only time your brother beat you up?"

"No. Anytime Dad was out of the house, Frank would find fault with something I'd done or, hell, something someone else had done, and he'd take it out on me. I was planning on leaving anyway. I was looking for a place. I just hadn't found one I could afford yet on the little my dad was paying me."

"But now you're safe. You're at Kirk's and everyone will look out for you."

"Yeah, as long as Frank doesn't find out where I am."

"Are you worried about it if he does?"

"Yeah. He won't like it that I'm happy. He doesn't just hate me. He despises me. I woke up one time to him holding a knife in front of my face. I yelled and Dad heard and came to my room. Before I could say anything, Frank told him I was being a wuss and having nightmares after the scary movie we'd all watched after dinner. Dad didn't let me say anything, just gave me a dirty look and told me to 'man up' before he left the room."

"Wow. Your brother sounds like a psychopath."

"Unfortunately," Lee said with a grimace. "Still think dating me is a good idea?"

"Well, since I'm planning to date you and not your brother, I think it sounds like a fantastic idea."

They were interrupted by their dinner being brought by the waitress.

"Wow… This looks amazing, although I don't think I can eat all this. That's a lot of steak."

"Don't worry about it. You might surprise yourself. The steaks here are fantastic."

Lee moaned after his first bite. It had simply melted in his mouth. He looked up quickly at the weird noise that had come from across the table. Lee was shocked to see the look Saul was giving him. It was a look of complete starvation — and not for food. Lee took a fast sip of his soda, flailing for a new topic of conversation.

"You were going to tell me about your crush in college," he said.

Saul reached up and scratched the back of his head in obvious discomfort. "I was really hoping you would forget about that."

"Well, it's only fair. You got to hear all about my drama."

Saul gave a very put-upon sigh before caving and telling the story. "I had this crush on this guy who was older than me by a couple years and on the football team. Man, he was gorgeous. I swear I thought he was putting the moves on me — always patting my ass, hugging me. I obsessed about him for weeks. I talked Eric's ear off about him and finally decided with me being me and not lacking in self-confidence…" Saul paused to wait for Lee to stop laughing. "As I was saying, I decided he would be lucky to have me and to take him up on his offer. I got all dressed up on Valentine's Day, grabbed some beer and headed to his off-campus apartment. Imagine my surprise when his girlfriend answered the door. They were heading out to dinner. I think I stuttered some excuse about not realizing he had a girlfriend and would have plans. At that point, the girlfriend got pissed because she thought he hadn't been telling people he was taken. So there he was glaring at me, trying to placate the girlfriend. He reached over, took the beer from me, said he would see me at practice and shut the door in my face."

Lee started laughing again, picturing the scene described. "Oh, man, how did he treat you the next time he saw you?"

"He cames up to me, said, *'Thanks for the beer,'* patted my ass and walked off."

"Really? He didn't say anything else?"

"Nope. And I learned an important lesson of not assuming that all straight boys know boundaries."

"Oh, that is classic. Eric knew you were gay?"

"Yeah. He was supposed to be gone one weekend and walked in on me and some guy I'd picked up at the club. Talk about awkward. Eric was always cool about it, though, mainly because he was bi himself."

"I wondered about that. Was he married before?"

"Yeah. He and his wife met in college. It was love at first sight for him. It took him a little while to convince her that he meant it, though. They were great together. Claire is a mini her. Absolutely fearless. His wife died of cancer several years ago. That was a very tough time." Saul looked haunted for a moment.

"But now he has Kirk." Saul's expression immediately brightened.

"Yep, now he has Kirk and they're also great together. It's different from Eric and Elizabeth, but Eric is a different person now. Before Elizabeth's death, he was fearless and invincible. When he found out Lizzie was pregnant, oh, man, he had a major strut going on." Saul chuckled as he obviously was reliving the moment before growing serious again. "They diagnosed her with ovarian cancer right after Claire was born. She fought so hard for several years. Eric was a trooper. I was gone for most of the end, playing ball, so I couldn't help as much as I wanted." Saul shrugged. "I did what I could. My mama came out to take care of Claire at the end so Eric could be at the hospital. Eric's mom caught the shingles and couldn't help the way she'd wanted. Man, did Eric's mom feel bad about that. The timing was horrible, but my mama just hopped on a plane and came as soon as she found out. I adore that woman." A genuine smile crossed his face as Saul talked about his mother, making Lee acutely miss his own.

Lee pushed those feelings aside as Saul continued his story. "And now he has Kirk. It's wonderful to see Eric happy again."

"You're buying Eric's house for your mama, right? You said she loves Eric's house?"

"Yes, as I said, she stayed with Claire there while Elizabeth was in the hospital that last time. She comes to visit me and Lexie a lot. This will make it easier for her and my dad."

"Oh, your dad is still alive?" A flush came up his face after he realized how bad that sounded. "Sorry. That didn't come out right. You just haven't talked about him much."

Saul chuckled. "No, it's all right. My dad is very laid-back. He kind of gets lost in the shuffle of all the extroverts in the family. He and my sister Lucia just sit back and let everyone else talk. The house will be good for him to have a place to escape. Lexie's boys can be a handful. He always looks exhausted when it's time to leave."

"What about you?"

"What about me?"

"Do you want kids one day?"

"You know it's weird. Being gay, I'd never really thought about it. I just had it in my head that I'm gay and I'm never going to have kids. You know what I mean?"

"Yeah," Lee answered with a sigh. "It was the one thing about being gay that made me wish I wasn't, not that I have a great role model from my own father — other than knowing how *not* to treat your kids."

"I do have a great role model in my father," Saul said, "and things are different than they were, even five years ago. Lately, I've been revisiting it in my brain. I mean, there's no reason I can't be a father one day. I would like to have a partner, of course, but I have the money. I can certainly hire a surrogate."

"Well, money is one thing I don't have, but I do want to one day as well. My mom taught me a lot about being a great parent, even if my father didn't. I feel like I have a lot of love to give. Will has certainly been a great role model for me, too." Lee shrugged. "Man, we're hitting all the serious subjects tonight."

"Yeah, we are, but it's not a bad thing. It's best to get these things out in the open at the beginning, don't you think?" Saul asked.

"You're right. I guess that's what dating is about — finding where you are compatible and where you aren't."

"That's the spirit. And speaking of dating... While we're dating, I would really like it to be just you and me, if that's okay? During my last and, honestly, only relationship, I didn't spell it out and he thought it meant it was okay for him to see other people whenever I was out of town. That's not how I operate," Saul said.

"Well, you don't have to worry about me on that front. I certainly don't want to date anyone else, in the first place, and I am way too shy to do anything like that, in the second place."

"Just wanted to make sure we were on the same page."

The waitress chose that moment to approach the table.

"Anything else I can get you, gentlemen?"

Lee was surprised to realize he had eaten everything on his plate while they'd been talking. He also realized he was almost unpleasantly full. He groaned. "I should've stopped eating like six bites ago."

"I'm guessing I can't interest you in any dessert then?" the waitress asked with a smile and a wink.

"Definitely none for me." Lee was quick to answer.

Saul chuckled. "None for me either. Just the check, when you have a minute."

"Gotcha. Will that be one check or two?"

"One please," Saul answered before Lee could even open his mouth.

"Great. I'll be right back with that."

Saul gave Lee a stern look. "It's a date. I asked. I'm paying."

"Okay. Well, next time I pay."

"Deal."

After the credit card slip was signed, Saul escorted Lee from the restaurant with a hand at his back. Just as they made it to the door, Lee heard his name called.

"Stuart!" Lee recognized the man who'd commissioned the artwork on his bike, right before he was engulfed in a hug.

"Good to see you, man. Where've you been? I went back looking to have you do another bike for me, but they just said you were gone. Couldn't tell me where."

"I'm at a different garage now. Everyone's Mechanic in Raleigh, off Falls of Neuse."

"Oh, wow. I've heard great things about that place. Well, as I said, I have another bike I'd like you to do — one for my brother. He loved what you did on mine."

"Well, bring it in. I'm sure Kirk will be fine with it. Kirk's the owner."

"Is this Kirk…? Wait, you're Saul Valencia. Great to meet you, man." Stuart reached out with his right arm, keeping his left arm across Lee's shoulders, and shook Saul's hand. "How do you know Lee here?"

"His boss is engaged to my best friend."

"Well, that's awesome. Guys night out?"

Lee didn't understand the look that came into Stuart's eyes as he asked the question, and he was definitely confused by the tightening of Stuart's grip on his shoulders. Saul seemed to understand what the look meant, though, and obviously didn't like it, because after releasing the handshake, he reached over and grabbed Lee's hand and pulled him in front of him — Lee's back to his chest — and wrapped both arms around him.

"Oh, it's like that, is it?"

"It's like that."

Stuart raised both hands in the air in an 'I surrender' pose. "I get it. He's a great guy. You're lucky."

"I know."

"Well, gotta go, I guess my table is ready," Stuart said while indicating the group of men waiting by the podium. "I'll bring the bike in soon. My brother's fortieth birthday is coming up. I want to get it done beforehand."

"Sounds good. See you soon," Lee told him.

Lee turned to Saul as soon as Stuart had gone. "What just happened?"

"You don't know?" Saul steered Lee through the door and to his SUV, opening the passenger door for him when they got there.

"Not a clue. It's why I asked."

Saul gave a 'just a minute' signal with his finger before walking around the vehicle and climbing into the driver's side. "Stuart wants you for more than just painting the bike."

"He does? Really?" Lee was honestly shocked.

Saul looked across the vehicle at him and started laughing. "You're too cute. You had no clue he was hitting on you just then?"

"What? Stuart's gay?"

Saul reached over and grabbed Lee by the arm. After pulling him so they met halfway over the armrest, he gave him an all-too-brief kiss before leaning back behind the wheel. "I'm obviously going to have to keep my eye on you to make sure no one comes in to poach you."

"I already told you that you don't have to worry about that."

"I know." With a chuckle, Saul started the vehicle. "So, what do you think we should do with the grassy area between the buildings?"

Chapter Five

"Lee! Watch what you're doing, boy." Will's sharp tone of voice snapped Lee out of his whirling thoughts more than the actual words.

"What?" Lee looked down to where he was about to step in a puddle of oil that had spilled on the floor. "Oh, crap. Sorry, Will."

"What's going on with you? You've been out of it all day today."

"Nothing. It's nothing."

"Yeah and you have a bridge to sell me too."

"Lee." Kirk's voice snapped out over the garage. "Get your butt in here."

"Boss man is calling. Maybe he can figure out what the hell is wrong with you."

Lee gave Will an apologetic look before making his way across the garage to Kirk.

"Go in and have a seat. I'll be right with you."

Lee sank into the chair in front of Kirk's desk to the ominous sound of the door closing. At least it sounded ominous to him at that moment.

"Okay. Out with it. What's going on with you? You haven't had your head in the game all day. I would think you'd be happy. You finished up Stuart Woods' bike and earned yourself a nice bonus at the same time."

Lee stared at his hands twisting in his lap. "It's nothing to do with work. I love it here, I swear."

"Then what is it? Let me help if I can. If it's not work, is it something to do with Saul? I thought things have been going well these last six weeks?"

"They are, I mean I *think* they are. Oh hell, I don't know anymore."

"Care to elaborate on that? I can't do anything with 'yes', 'no', 'maybe'."

"The last six weeks have been good. We've become really good friends and we've done some really amazing and fun things on the weekends, but —"

When it became obvious Lee wasn't going to continue, Kirk prompted him, "But…"

"I don't think he's interested in me for anything more."

Kirk scoffed. "Yeah, that's why I've caught him on several occasions with his tongue down your throat…because he's not interested."

Lee replied, "When I'm at the office and working on the mural or we're somewhere else in public is the only time he touches me, though. I asked him to come over to watch a movie with me last night after I put the finishing touches on the mural at the office, hoping he would get the hint that I wanted to move things forward."

Kirk interrupted him to say. "It looks fantastic, by the way. I saw it at lunch."

Lee smiled at that. He was quite proud of how it had turned out.

"Sorry. I didn't mean to interrupt. What happened last night?"

"Nothing."

"What do you mean 'nothing'?" Kirk asked, obviously confused.

"I mean, Saul came over and sat in the freaking recliner rather than next to me on the couch. Then" — Lee's voice rose but he couldn't do anything about it in his current tangled, emotionally messy mood — "then he kissed me on the forehead before he left. On the freaking *forehead*!"

Kirk raised his hand to his mouth in a very poor attempt to hide the smirk on his face. At Lee's glare, he changed it to a cough. "Have you tried coming right out and saying you're ready to move this relationship along?"

"And how exactly do I do that? Hey, Saul, I'm tired of this slow crap. Meet me in the bedroom and bang me."

Kirk laughed outright now.

"It's not funny."

"It kinda is. How about this… Saul's at work. Why don't you head over there and talk to him?" Kirk raised his hand to stop Lee from speaking when he opened his mouth. "Just ask him where he sees the relationship going. Tell him you're ready for the next step."

"You make it sound so easy."

"I seem to remember us having this conversation before."

"I know. I know. What about work?"

"I think we can manage to finish up without you today. Just come back focused on Monday. I think part of the problem is that you're working way too hard and you're exhausted. You've been working on the mural at the store on Monday, Wednesday and Friday and on the house mural on Tuesdays and Thursdays, now that the Andersons have moved out. Between that, working full-time here and starting a relationship, you're running on empty."

"I can't argue with you on that. It's been a lot. I've been happy, though, other than this one thing."

"Yeah, '*this one thing*'. Go talk to him."

"Yes, sir."

* * * *

"Really? Stephanie said 'yes'? She's finally taking pity on you and marrying you? That's awesome, man. Congratulations."

Saul reached out and pulled his former teammate and another of his best friends into his arms for a quick hug, then slapped him on the back before putting him at arm's length to grin down at him. A gasp had him turning towards the open doorway.

"Lee!"

"Well, I guess that answers the question of why you aren't interested in me anymore."

With that, Lee spun and headed back out of the door.

"What? Lee! Come back!"

Saul rushed out of the door after him and reached the parking lot just in time to see Lee peel out of his parking space. Eric came up behind him.

"Was that Lee? Why did he leave in such a hurry?"

"I have no idea. Brian was just telling me Stephanie said 'yes'. I was congratulating him and giving him a hug, when Lee came in. He said something about answering the question of why I wasn't interested then he bolted."

"Where would he get the idea that you weren't interested anymore?"

"No clue."

"Hang on. Let me call Kirk and see if he knows what's going on."

Saul waited as Eric called Kirk. A lot of 'uh-huhs' and 'what's' from Eric's side of the conversation didn't help him at all. Eric ended the call with a 'let us know if he comes back there' before putting his phone back in his pocket.

"Did you really sit in the recliner at his apartment when he invited you over for a movie last night?"

"Um...yeah. I'm taking it slow like everyone told me to do, even if it's killing me."

"Six weeks isn't moving slow. That's glacial. Lee thinks you aren't interested in him that way anymore. He says that the only touching you do is in public. Any truth to *that*?" Eric's emphasis on the word 'that' and the raised eyebrow told him the real answer wasn't going to be a popular one.

"I don't trust myself in private. I want him so badly, but I don't want to rush him."

"So instead, you've made him feel like you don't want him at all. Great job, man. He invited you to watch a movie. Did you really think he wanted to watch a movie? Were you waiting for him to announce over the PA system at the store that he was ready to move forward or something?"

"Ugh, I'm such an idiot. I have to find him."

"Everything okay out here?" Brian interrupted from behind them.

"No. My boyfriend thinks I'm cheating on him with you."

Brian started to laugh, abruptly stopping when Eric and Saul just stared at him. "Oh. You're serious."

"Yep. I guess I haven't been paying enough attention to his signals. God! I suck at this dating thing." Saul reached up, grabbed two handfuls of his hair and pulled.

"Huh," Brian said.

"Huh, what?" Saul asked.

"Never thought I would see the day somebody had you in knots. Usually you've kept yourself separate."

"Well, Lee is special. I want it all with him."

"And have you mentioned this to him? And if he's so important, why haven't I met him?" Brian continued with another judgmental eyebrow lift.

Saul just screamed to the sky, then flipped off his two best friends as they laughed at him.

* * * *

"Still no sign of him?" Will's voice made Saul jump where he was sitting in front of the door to Lee's apartment.

Saul glared at Will. "No. And he's not answering his phone either," Saul said out loud, before mumbling under his breath, "any of the thirty times I've tried. Have you tried calling him?"

"I did. He didn't answer me either. Did you leave him a voicemail, explaining?"

"Yes, I did. I hope he listens to it and gives me another chance."

"I'm sure he will. You just have to give him time to calm down. He has to know in his heart that you aren't the type to cheat on him."

"I hope so."

"How did he not recognize Brian, anyway?"

Saul grimaced. "Because I haven't actually introduced him to anyone yet. I wanted to give him time to get used to me first. What?" he asked at Will's pitying look.

"You have to realize by now that Lee is an all-in kind of guy. He puts his heart and soul into everything he does. You not making a move and you not introducing him to your friends — or I'm guessing family — would be signs to him that you aren't."

Saul hung his head. "I really didn't realize so much time had passed. I was just going moment to moment. He's been so busy between painting and here. I was just enjoying having him to myself the other times, despite what my blue balls have been telling me," Saul finished with a self-deprecating laugh.

"I get it. I do. Lee is a great guy and you didn't want to scare him off, but you need to make a move now or you're going to lose him."

"First I have to find him."

"Well, you can't wait here any longer. We're locking up for the weekend. Go home. Maybe he'll come to you there. I'll let you know if I hear anything and I'm sure Eric and Kirk will as well."

Saul groaned as he took the hand Will offered to help him up. The stoop in front of Lee's door was not the most comfortable place in the world to be. He'd checked the roof, but Lee was not in his painting area, as he'd hoped. Saul dejectedly took himself home, stopping to grab takeout since he didn't trust his ability to focus on cooking. He spent the evening alternating between staring at his phone and pacing, sometimes both at the same time before forcing himself to go to bed. He thought he must have slept, but he woke exhausted from the tossing and turning with worry.

The next morning found him knocking on Eric and Kirk's door. "Any word?" he asked Eric as soon as the door opened.

"No. Come on in, man. You look like hell."

"I feel like hell. His truck still isn't at the garage. Where could he have gone?"

"I don't know, man, but he'll show up."

"But what if?" Saul asked, lowering his voice to a whisper. "What if he went out and found someone new?"

"I highly doubt that," Eric said with a chuckle. "You *have* met him, right?"

Saul ran his hand through his hair for the thousandth time since Lee had run out of his office the previous day.

"Come on. We just finished breakfast. There're leftovers. I made cinnamon buns today. You need to eat something."

Saul let himself be led to the kitchen where Kirk was sipping a cup of coffee and Claire was sitting at the breakfast bar coloring.

"Hey, what happened to all the cinnamon buns? I thought there were six left? Where did the other four go?"

Claire answered, "Sam took some over to Lee."

"What?" all three adults asked her at once, making her jump.

Claire looked up in shock at the three men. Eric was the first to recover.

"What do you mean she took some over to Lee, sweetie?"

"We can see the new playroom window from Sam's room. The light came on last night. That means Lee is over there working on our painting. Sam was worried that he didn't eat, so she took some over to him."

"And where were you while this was all decided?" Eric asked Kirk.

"I ran to the bathroom. She was gone when I came back. I assumed — wrongly, it appears — that she'd gone to her room for something." Turning to Claire, he added, "While it is very nice you guys are looking out for Lee, we're going to be having a long discussion about just leaving the house without telling anyone where you're going."

"She did tell someone. She told me," Claire responded.

Eric reached out and tugged on the end of Claire's braid. "An adult someone."

"Oh. Sorry."

Kirk stood up, taking a final sip of his coffee before setting his cup on the counter. "Let me grab my shoes and I'll walk over with you and grab my kid so you and Lee can talk."

"Sounds good." It took all Saul had to wait for Kirk and not bolt on out.

As they opened the door, they startled Eric's mother as she was getting ready to ring the doorbell on the other side of it.

"Hi, Mama H. You're early."

"Yeah. Traffic was light for once. Made it here without any slowdowns."

"Well, Eric and Claire are in the kitchen. Sam has done a walkabout and has gone over to see Lee at the new house. We'll be right back. Thank you so much for watching the girls for a few hours today so Eric and I can go out to lunch."

"You know I adore those two. We're going to be girly and go get pedicures."

"Oh, I'm sure they will love that."

Saul ran out of patience. Leaning down, he kissed Eric's mother on the cheek. "Great to see you, but I need to go talk to Lee."

"Right. Sam and I will be right back."

Saul was vibrating with tension as Kirk jogged to catch up with him. He hurried down the street and around the corner to the cul-de-sac that ran behind Eric's current house, where their new house was located.

"Tell me," Kirk huffed, "why didn't Lee recognize Brian? You guys have been dating, what? Six weeks? He didn't recognize one of your best friends?"

"I haven't introduced Lee to my friends yet. Don't look at me like that. They know about him. I just wanted him all to myself a little longer. You know how our friend group can be."

"Yeah. Obnoxious and nosy as hell."

"Exactly. I mean, I adore every one of the assholes, but I wanted to ease Lee into things."

"And what about your family? You have at least introduced him to your sister, right?"

At Saul's wince, Kirk exploded. "For fuck's sake, man!"

"I know, I know. I screwed up, okay? I'm going to fix it, though. *All* of it. *If* he gives me a chance."

Kirk scoffed. "He adores you. He'll give you another chance, but you're going to have to work hard to regain his trust. Don't get me wrong. Eric and I will confirm to him that it was just Brian, not a love interest, but he has already started from a place where he didn't think he was good enough for you."

"I know." Saul lengthened his stride to get to Lee faster.

"Hold up, asshole. My legs aren't as long as yours."

Saul's response was to give Kirk the finger as he stepped up onto the porch.

"Nice. Real nice."

As they opened the door and stepped inside the house, they could hear Sam talking to Lee.

"Lee?"

"Yeah, Sam?"

"Do Daddies love their little girls the most?"

"Yep. That's what they say."

"Oh." Kirk and Saul both paused as they heard the sadness in the little girl's voice.

"Why the long face? You have two great dads."

"No, I don't," Sam snapped. "I have uncles. I heard Eric and Uncle Kirk talking. Uncle Kirk is going to adopt Claire after they get married, so Claire will have two daddies who love her best. When Eric asked what they were going to do about me, Uncle Kirk said they would have to see. He's not going to send me away, is he, Lee?"

The two men shared a look of horror before Kirk sprinted up the stairs upon hearing Sam burst into tears. Saul followed close behind and stopped once he entered the room, watching as Kirk dropped to the floor in front of Sam and pulled her into his arms, where she completely fell apart.

"Baby, please don't cry. I would never send you away. You're my angel. You can't get rid of me."

Saul's gaze went to Lee where he was sitting on the floor leaning against the wall. Kirk and Sam were on the floor directly in front of him. Lee's own tear-filled eyes met Saul's before he quickly looked down at his lap.

Turning to Saul, Kirk mouthed, "Call Eric."

With something to do, Saul stepped out into the hall and called Eric. Saul didn't even wait for Eric to say anything beyond the word 'hey'.

"Eric, you need to get over here ASAP."

"Why? What's wrong?"

"Just leave Claire with your mom and get over here. Sam is crying, asking about you guys sending her away because daddies love their little girls best. She overheard you asking Kirk to adopt Claire."

"What does that have to do with sending...? You know what? Never mind. I'm on my way." Saul heard Eric yelling for his mom and asking her to keep Claire there as he hung up the phone.

"He's on his way," Saul called to Kirk. Less than a minute later, the door downstairs crashed open and Eric came bounding up the stairs, two at a time. By this time, Sam's sobs were down to occasional whimpers. While Saul had been gone, Lee must have raided the stash of supplies in the corner to grab paper towels, because he was just handing the roll to Kirk as he and Eric came through the door.

Lee hesitated a moment then ripped a couple of paper towels off the roll before completing the transfer to Kirk. Lee passed by Saul to go to the bathroom across the hall with a muttered 'excuse me' — but no eye contact. The water turned on then off a few seconds later. Lee had obviously decided a damp paper towel was needed because he walked back and handed it to

Eric, where he was on the floor next to Kirk, rubbing Sam's back.

"Now, what's this all about, sweetie?" Kirk asked. "You know Eric and I both love you very much. Why would you think we would send you away?"

"Be-be-cause—" Sam began taking gasping breaths in between the stuttering syllables. "You want to be Claire's papa and not mi-mine. You just want to be my un-uncle. Everyone says daddies love their daughters more than anyone. So, you must love Claire mo-more."

"Oh, Sammy, that's just not true. I love all three of you so much. There is no difference in the amount. You never asked about calling me 'Papa'. I didn't want to take the place of your daddy."

"But you do all the things a daddy does." Sam's voice got even lower as she continued, more tears leaking from her eyes. "And Mrs. Jackson says that since I'm not your daughter, they should take me away from you and the bad house."

"Wait! Your teacher, Mrs. Jackson, said that to you?" Eric asked, pausing his hand in the rubbing of her back.

Sam nodded, bobbing her head up and down. "She said our house was against the will of God and that I should never have been allowed to stay with you. It was one thing when it was separate houses, but now that we'll all be living together, something should be done." Kirk and Eric shared a look that promised retribution in a very painful way on this Mrs. Jackson. Sam obviously thought they were mad at her, though, because she flinched back.

Kirk took a deep breath, obviously pushing down his anger and pulled Sam back into a hug. "I'm not mad at you. Understand? Mrs. Jackson was wrong to say what she did, and I *will* be talking to her and the principal about it tomorrow. Okay?"

Sam nodded and burrowed into Kirk's arms.

"And if it's what you want," Kirk began, raising her chin to look her in the eyes, "I would love for you to call me 'Papa'. You know your mom had me adopt you as a condition of the will, because she didn't want there to be any problems for you. I already think of you as mine. I thought you knew that and understood."

"Really? You're okay with me calling you 'Papa'?" Such expressions of hope and joy were almost painful to watch, and Saul found himself swallowing down the emotion that threatened to choke him.

"I would love that more than anything."

"Do you think Mommy and Daddy would mind?"

"No, I don't think they would mind. I'll be your papa. They will always be your mommy and daddy."

"I don't really remember them much anymore. Just little things, like Mommy loving flowers and working in the garden and Daddy lying in his hammock. That's why I asked Lee to paint them in the picture. See?" She pointed at the mural on the wall behind Kirk and Eric. "So I can see them and remember."

Saul's gaze went to the painting for the first time. He'd thought the phrase 'jaw dropping' was something that never actually happened, but he had to remember to close his mouth with a snap. It was amazing. Fred the dragon was there, flying over the castle. Sam was there in her princess-knight gear. An entire kingdom laid out to be explored.

Lee walked over to the mural and pointed to where Sam's mom and dad were painted. Her dad was in a hammock with her mom showing him some flowers she was getting ready to plant.

Lee said, "Um, Sam gave me a picture she had of her parents. She was upset when, after the Anderson's moved into her old house, Mrs. Anderson took out all the flowers her mother had planted to put in a Koi pond, , so we added her parents and the flowers to the mural. And yeah, Claire's mom is up here." Lee pointed up at a cloud where an angel was sitting, playing a harp or lute or whatever they were called. Saul could never remember. "Hope that's okay?"

"Okay?" Eric stood up to pull Lee into a hug. "It's more than okay. This is absolutely fantastic." Turning back to Sam, he added, "But, sweetie, why didn't you tell us you were upset about the flowers? Why didn't you tell us about any of this? It's not okay for Mrs. Jackson — or anyone, for that matter — to make you feel bad. That's why we're here. We're your parents." Eric closed his eyes and sighed. "But you didn't feel we were your parents, did you? Oh, sweetie." Eric reached out and pulled Sam up and into his arms for a hug. "Know this. As soon as Kirk and I tie the knot, I'm filing papers to adopt you too. Understood? As far as I'm concerned, I'm lucky enough to have two daughters. Got it?"

Sam nodded her head where she had it buried in the crook of his neck.

"Now I think it's time for us to go home and go out for a family lunch. What do you say?"

Sam nodded again but tightened her arms around Eric's neck when he tried to set her down, so he just kept her in his arms and headed for the door. Kirk stood and went first to Lee.

"This painting is amazing, Lee. I'm awed by your talent and I will be spending a *lot* of time in the future finding all the things in it, but right now I hope you understand that I have family time to enjoy and you have some things of your own to work out." Kirk put his hands on Lee's shoulders. "It's not what you think. Listen to him. Give him a chance to explain."

Lee looked to Saul before dropping his gaze back to stare at the floor again, giving Kirk a nod. With a final shake, Kirk let go of Lee, turned and headed to the door.

Stopping in front of Saul, he said, for Saul's ears only, "Don't fuck this up again."

Saul nodded. Kirk must have seen he meant it because he patted him on the shoulder before he walked out of the door, following Eric and Sam.

Chapter Six

Lee couldn't bring himself to look at Saul. He'd had an epiphany, a painful one at that, at, like, three o'clock in the morning. Saul wouldn't cheat. There had to be a logical explanation, but right now Lee already felt like he had been wrung out like a dirty dishrag. Between the fretting, the anger and hurt, and the painting marathon the previous night as he'd worked through his emotions, Lee didn't think he'd slept more than four hours in the last two nights. Sam had, in fact, woken him up bringing him the cinnamon buns. He'd felt very ill-equipped to deal with her tears and had been so thankful when Kirk had burst through the door.

"Um, would you like a cinnamon bun? Sam brought them for me," Lee asked quietly.

"Could you look at me, please?"

Lee sensed more than saw Saul come closer to him, until Saul's shoes appeared in his line of sight. He sighed before looking up at Saul. "I know you wouldn't cheat. It's not who you are."

"But I haven't made you secure in our relationship. That was my friend Brian, by the way. He finally talked his girlfriend into agreeing to marry him."

A flush rose up Lee's cheeks. "Oh, I feel even worse now." Saul had talked a lot about his friend Brian. Saul reached out and pulled Lee into his arms. He rested his head on Saul's shoulder and let himself just be held for a moment.

"Don't. Don't feel bad. You would've known who he was if I hadn't been keeping you to myself. Eric said you thought I was hiding you and didn't want to introduce you to my friends and family. That is so not true. I just didn't want to scare you away. And as far as not wanting you?" Saul pressed Lee's hips to his, where Lee couldn't miss the rather large bulge pressing into him. "I want you bad, and my control has been fraying, which is why I sat in the recliner…like an idiot. You tried to tell me. I missed all the signs."

"Maybe we can both do better at this communicating thing. If you still want to be with me, that is?"

Saul raised Lee's chin and looked him in the eye. "I don't plan to ever let you go. You're mine. You'd better get used to it, which means we have dinner tonight at my sister's house in" — Saul grabbed his phone from his pocket and looked at the time — "eight hours. You up for it?"

Lee winced. "Maybe after a nap. I'm exhausted." Lee paused then said, "Would you like to come back to my apartment with me for a nap? Nothing else, sadly. When we do get together, I actually want to enjoy it, and I'm running on fumes right now." Lee punctuated his statement with a big yawn before dropping his head again to Saul's shoulder.

"I didn't sleep much last night either. A nap back at your apartment sounds perfect, but, Lee" — Saul waited until Lee raised his head to look at him again — "you can't run away from me anymore. If we have a problem, we talk it out. It about killed me when I couldn't find you and you didn't go home or answer your phone. Promise me. Throw things at me, yell at me, but don't just disappear."

"I promise. I'm sorry I worried you." Lee took a step back and patted his pockets. "I honestly don't even know where my phone is at the moment. I probably left it in the truck."

"Yeah. Well, we'll grab it on the way out. You're way too tired to drive yourself. We can get your car later or tomorrow after work. I'm not letting you out of my sight until I have to on Monday morning."

* * * *

Lee woke with a start when he tried to roll over and found he couldn't move. Glancing down, he saw the arm wrapped around him, holding him tight to the warm body behind him. Lee relaxed as he remembered returning to his apartment to nap with Saul. Lee squirmed, trying to get more comfortable as he realized his arm was asleep beneath him.

"Sleeping here," a grumbly voice said from behind him.

"Well, I need you to loosen up a little so I can get in a different position, big guy. My arm is asleep."

A chuckle blew warm air into his ear, giving him goosebumps, before Saul raised his arm so Lee could roll over to face him. Lee then pushed on Saul's shoulder to encourage him to lie flat. Lee lifted then sprawled across Saul's chest while shaking out his tingly arm. Saul reached up and rubbed his hand up and down Lee's arm to help get the circulation flowing again. After a few moments, the sensation finally eased up and he relaxed further onto Saul's chest. His very naked chest. *Holy shit!* How had he not remembered Saul taking off his shirt? Lee realized that he himself was in his underwear and he groaned.

"What?" Saul asked.

"I'm guessing you undressed me because I certainly don't remember much after getting in your truck to come here."

"Yeah and? You were really out of it."

"Because I don't remember it! The first time you strip clothes off me, and I don't remember it. That's just wrong on so many levels."

"Well, nothing happened. We just slept."

"I wasn't accusing you of anything. I know you're a gentleman. The last six weeks have certainly proven that. I'm just sorry I missed it."

"Oh, sorry," Saul said with an adorable, sheepish look. "I'm just feeling a little raw yet."

"Well, you need to stop. We said we were going to make this work. Right?"

"Right," Saul answered with conviction and a squeeze of his arms.

Lee leaned up and kissed him. What he meant to be a quick peck quickly morphed into something a little more frantic. "Please tell me we have time before we have to be at your sister's?"

"What sister?" Saul moaned, pushing Lee's head back down for another mind-numbing kiss. The alarm going off on Saul's phone interrupted them just as Lee had finally worked up the nerve to run his hands over

Saul's chest. They pulled apart with a groan. Lee rolled off Saul and onto his back as Saul reached for his phone on the bedside table.

"Why did I call my sister and tell her I was bringing you tonight? I should have canceled altogether."

Saul's whiny tone made Lee laugh. "Yeah, well, you did, and she was way too excited about it for us to cancel now. What time is it anyway?"

"Four-thirty."

"What time do we have to be at your sister's?"

"Six-thirty. We might be late," Saul said as he tossed the phone back on the bedside table.

"What? Why?" Lee jerked his head around to look at Saul just as Saul rolled over on top of him, rolling his hips to grind their underwear-covered erections together.

Lee groaned, wrapping his arms around Saul's neck as Saul mauled his mouth in another heated kiss. Saul pulled back just enough to reach between them and yank Lee's underwear down to mid-thigh then push his own down and off. Saul's cock was a thing of beauty, definitely in proportion to the big man's size. Lee reached out and ran his finger over the tip of Saul's cock to catch a drop of pre-cum that was about to drip off. Raising the finger to his lips, he sucked it, groaning at his first taste.

"Oh, that's good." Lee reached for another sample, but Saul grabbed his hand and placed it over his head. Lee looked up at Saul in surprise. "What?"

Saul groaned. "If you do that again, this may be over way too quickly."

Saul rolled them both to their sides facing each other. Lee watched in fascination as Saul licked his palm and grabbed both of their cocks in one of his large, slightly callused hands, which felt amazing on his cock. Lee arched into Saul before forcing his hips back slightly so he could watch. The contrast in skin color of Saul's olive-toned skin and his own pale tone was amazingly erotic.

Then Saul added a twist at the top of his stroke and Lee stopped thinking altogether. His entire world centered on Saul's touch. Lee started rubbing his hand over Saul's muscular chest. Saul's guttural groan as Lee pinched his nipple had Lee looking back up into Saul's eyes. Keeping eye contact, Lee leaned forward and closed his lips around the rigid nub and sucked before lightly nipping at it. Lee was rewarded with another guttural groan before Saul grabbed him by the hair at the back of his head and pulled him into another heated kiss. Lee continued to run his hand over Saul's chest, rubbing and alternating pinches between both nipples.

Saul released his grip on their cocks, pressed Lee onto his back and lowered his body fully onto Lee's, the better to grind their cocks together. He dropped his forehead to rest it on Lee's shoulder, which seemed to get him better leverage. Moments later, Lee felt Saul's release on his belly and the heat of Saul's cum on his cock was enough to send Lee over the edge too.

Lee wrapped both arms around Saul as he panted, waiting for his heart rate to come down enough so he could speak. "Wow," was all he managed.

Saul chuckled and lifted his head to give Lee a peck on the lips. "Wow, indeed." Another alarm went off on Saul's phone. With a groan he lifted off Lee and again grabbed his phone from the bedside table to silence it, snagging a couple of tissues from the box behind it afterward for cleanup. He wiped at the mess on Lee's stomach before chuckling and looking up at him.

"While that took a little bit of the edge off, that alarm meant that we really do need to get going or we're going to be late, especially as I think we're going to have to jump into the shower. These tissues just aren't cutting it, I'm afraid." Leaning in, Saul gave Lee another quick peck but pulled back before anything else could happen. Patting Lee's hip, Saul climbed out of bed then offered Lee a hand. Lee took a moment to finish removing his boxers and swiping at more of the mess on his stomach before tossing them in the general direction of his hamper.

Lee felt Saul's gaze on him as he walked toward the bathroom. Looking over his shoulder, he saw Saul was watching his ass, not moving from his spot next to the bed. "You coming?"

"Man, I was a dumbass not getting you in my bed weeks ago. I have a feeling you're going to be addictive. I think it's going to have to be separate showers. I may make us very late if we're both wet and naked at the same time."

"Okay. I'll be quick." Lee hustled into the shower.

Lee returned to the room a few minutes later with a towel wrapped around his hips to find Saul sitting on his bed fully dressed. "I thought you were going to shower?"

"Actually, do you mind if we swing by my house? My clothes got pretty wrinkled and I don't want to show up at my sister's a mess. It's on the way. That way I can pack a bag to bring back for tonight."

"Are we having a sleepover?" Lee asked with a smirk over his shoulder at Saul as he went to his dresser for underwear, pulling them on under the towel before walking to his closet for a shirt and pants.

Saul stood from the bed and came to Lee, folding him into his arms. "Yep. I told you. I'm not letting you out of my sight until you have to go to work tomorrow morning. Do you have a problem with that?"

Lee pretended to think about it for a moment before answering with a grin. "Nope. None."

"Good. Then finish getting ready so we can go." After Lee was dressed, Saul grabbed his hand and they made their way out of the apartment to Saul's truck. Lee opened the gate and let Saul drive out before closing and locking the lot gate and hopping into the passenger side.

"You know, we could swing by and grab my truck from Kirk and Eric's house after dinner, since you all seem to live so close to each other. Then we won't have to run around in traffic tomorrow night. I could just make us something for dinner after you finish work that way."

"We'll see how late we finish," Saul replied.

Lee stared out of the window in silence as they drove to Saul's current condo, where he lived while he waited for his apartment above the offices to be completed.

"What's wrong?" Saul's voice suddenly broke the silence.

"Nothing." Lee hesitated a moment, after seeing the sharp disbelieving glance Saul threw him. Then he answered truthfully, "I'm just a little nervous about meeting your sister, I guess. Everything has changed so fast. I went from thinking we were breaking up to finally meeting your sister, not to mention what happened in between, all within a span of, like, twelve hours."

Saul reached over and grabbed Lee's hand, twining their fingers together. "I know — and I apologize again for not moving us forward."

"It wasn't just your fault, you know. I could've spoken up way before I reached my meltdown point."

"True, but as we said, we're both going to work on our communication, and we're going to make this work. I can't imagine my life without you in it anymore."

Lee flushed with pleasure. "Believe me… I feel the same."

"Good. Then stop worrying. My sister is going to love you."

After a quick stop at Saul's apartment, they made the drive to Saul's sister's house.

"Now, the husband is Matt, right?"

"Yep. Husband Matt, sons Andrew who is ten and Nicholas who is twelve. They're a hoot and they're going to love you too."

Exiting the truck, Saul came around and grabbed Lee's hand, leading him up the sidewalk to the front door. Saul shot Lee a quick grin and gave a squeeze of his hand before pushing the doorbell.

Lee jumped at the noise that erupted after the button was pushed. Dogs came rushing to the door and he heard a yelled "I got it" from one of the boys, followed by the sound of pounding feet.

"Uncle Saul!" the boy who answered the door screamed before launching himself at Saul. Saul dropped Lee's hand to catch him as the dogs wove in and out of Lee's and Saul's legs. Lee leaned down to pet the large dogs, who appeared to be some kind of Lab mix. The pats only seemed to drive them into greater levels of energy instead of calming them down, as Lee had hoped.

A female voice joined the mix. "Jake, Nilla… Inside *now*." The dogs gave Lee's fingers one more lick before rushing back inside.

Lee turned his attention in the direction of the voice then had to drop his gaze several inches. He didn't know why he'd thought Saul's sister would be tall too, but obviously that wasn't the case. Lexie appeared to only be a little over five feet tall.

"I know. I know. I'm the runt of the family. I always say Mom was saving the height for this one," Lexie said as she reached out her hand to Lee. "Hi. I'm Lexie. Welcome to the insane asylum. It's great to finally meet you, Lee."

Lee stuttered out a "Nice to meet you too" that ended in a yelp as Lexie used her handgrip to pull Lee into a hug. He raised his shocked gaze to Saul, who was standing there laughing at him.

"My family doesn't believe in formality. You might as well get used to it now. Here, take this sack of potatoes." Saul then handed Lee the boy in his arms, who he assumed was Andrew, before giving his sister a hug then going into the house.

"Hi. I'm Andy. Who are you?"

"Um, I'm Lee. Nice to meet you, Andy."

"Do you like Legos?"

"Does anyone *not* like Legos?"

"I don't when I step on them," Lexie answered. "Speaking of… Did you finish picking them up, young man?"

"Um… Let me go check really quick," Andy said as he wiggled to get down.

"That's what I thought."

"Where're Matt and Nick?"

"Nick is in the midst of science fair project hell. It's due tomorrow and my great procrastinator is in panic mode today. Matt is in the kitchen slicing some strawberries to go with dessert."

Suddenly a pained yelp rang out from somewhere to the left and Saul and Lexie took off at a run. Lee followed at a slower pace, since he didn't know where he was going. He reached the kitchen to see Saul and Lexie standing on either side of a blond man, presumably Matt. He was very striking between the dark Italian looks of his wife and brother-in-law. What really caught Lee's attention was the already-blood-soaked towel being wrapped around his hand.

"What happened?" Lexie asked.

"Forgot we got new knives yesterday. It worked a little too well."

"You were cutting the berries while holding them in your hand again, weren't you?"

Matt looked honestly bewildered. "How else do you cut strawberries?"

"On the cutting board?" Lexie asked, sarcasm dripping from her voice.

Saul interjected. "Here... Let's head to the sink and take a look." After unwrapping the towel, Saul swiped at it, wiping off the pooling blood to get a closer look.

"Ugh. Stop that. It hurts."

"I think you might actually need stitches this time, Matt."

Lexie turned to Lee. "Not quite how I meant this meeting to go, but this is my husband, Matt. He's a bit accident prone." The exasperation in her tone was evened out by the tenderness of her expression as she rubbed her hand up and down Matt's back.

"Hey. Lee, right?" Matt said, looking over his shoulder at Lee. "I'd shake your hand, but… *Ow!*" Matt whipped his head back around to watch what Saul was doing. "Will you quit poking at it, Saul?"

"Stop being such a wuss. It's definitely going to need stitches."

"Okay. I'll just drive myself to the urgent care."

"You will *not*," Saul and Lexie yelled together, making Lee and Matt both jump. Lee was just thankful he wasn't directly between the two of them, as Matt was presently, because that had to have been loud.

"Lexie can take you," Saul continued in a slightly softer tone of voice. "Lee and I can stay with the boys."

Lexie grabbed her purse off the counter. "Dinner is obviously delayed. I don't know how long we'll be. We were going to have steak and burgers, but why don't you order pizza or something? Do you remember which urgent care it was that was open late on Sunday?" The last question was aimed at her husband as she herded him out of the door.

"And that," Saul said with a laugh, "is my sister and her husband. I would like to say this is an unusual occurrence but it's not. Between Matt and the boys, they personally are paying for their doctors' respective beach houses. I swear."

Lee laughed as he was meant to then helped Saul clean up the kitchen.

"Well, it looks like he'd barely started with the strawberries, so there's not much to clean up, at least."

"Should we cut them up?"

"Naw. They'll stay fresher uncut. Let's just put them away."

Lee and Saul made quick work of putting the kitchen to rights then went in search of the boys. A thought struck Lee. "I'm really surprised the boys didn't come to check out what happened."

"They probably didn't even hear it, if they're up in the bonus room." Saul led Lee through the laundry room off the kitchen then up the stairs to the room over the garage. "See? With the laundry going, you can't hear much."

When they reached the top of the stairs, they saw Andy playing some kind of video game on the large TV mounted on the wall. Seated at one of those six-foot fold-up tables was Nick. Where Andy was a mix of both his parents, Nick was the spitting image of what Saul must have looked like at that age. When the boy saw Saul, he got up and came to give his uncle a big hug. He was still a foot or so shorter than Saul and at that awkward, gangly stage, but if the size of his feet were any indication, that wouldn't be the case for long.

"Hey, Nick. I'd like you to meet my boyfriend, Lee."

"Hi, Lee, nice to meet you."

Lee preened on the inside, being introduced as Saul's boyfriend, but outwardly he reached out his hand to shake. Nick seemed pleased by the gesture, puffing up his chest a little bit as they shook.

"Your mom had to take your dad to the urgent care to get his hand looked at. He cut himself with the new knives and is going to need stitches."

"Again?" Nick asked with an eyeroll.

Andy was quick to defend his dad. "Like you can talk. Mister I-Tripped-Over-a-Crack-in-the-Sidewalk-and-Broke-My-Finger-Catching-Myself."

Saul interrupted before it could become a full-out battle. "Well, I've been told to order pizza for dinner. Any preferences?"

After the dinner order was decided and placed, Saul said, "Okay. Dinner will be here in forty-five minutes or so." Saul turned to Nick again. "I hear you have your science fair project due tomorrow."

"Yeah. I have all the data and stuff, but I can't get it to look right. Everything looks stupid."

"I was actually pretty good at putting presentations together at school. Mind if I take a look?" Lee offered.

"Just don't do it for him or Lexie will have my head."

"Uncle Saul! Come play with me," Andy called.

Two and a half hours later, all four of them were on the floor, working to build a new Lego kit Andy had received for his birthday the month before, when Lexie and Matt came up the stairs to join them.

"Hello, boys."

"Mom! Dad!" Andy greeted them with the only volume Lee had heard him. *Loud*.

"How many stitches?" Saul asked as he got up to kiss his sister's cheek.

"Six. At least it's not his writing hand this time."

"That's a good thing."

"Look, Mom. Lee sorted all the parts so we can find them easier. We borrowed some of the plasticware stuff to keep them separated. Isn't that cool?"

Lee flushed. "Hope you don't mind."

"Not at all. Any way you can help keep the Legos under control is fine by me. Nicholas? Shouldn't you be working on your project?"

Nick didn't look up from where he was trying to fit two pieces together. "Already done. Lee helped me figure out how to make it so it didn't look lame."

"Not lame. High praise indeed." Matt wandered over to look at the finished product as he was speaking. A beat of silence followed by "Wow" had Lexie making her way over to look at it too, as Lee looked on anxiously.

"I didn't do it for him. I understand that's against the rules. I just gave him some ideas and cut out some of the stuff he used to glue onto the charts."

"It's fine," Lexie assured him.

"And done. Done is the important part," Matt added. "I thought for sure we were going to be up until midnight finishing this."

"He actually had all the data. He just had to put it together."

"Good job, team. Did you happen to save any pizza for us?" Lexie asked.

"What is this 'saving of pizza' of which you speak? Do people actually do that?" Saul asked his sister.

"Actually," Lee said with a laugh, "we ordered an extra pizza just for you guys. We figured you'd be hungry when you got back."

"My awesome man's idea." Saul came over to throw his arm across Lee's shoulders and gave him a peck on the cheek as he said it.

"Well, you paid for it," Lee said with a chuckle.

"Go team!" Andy yelled.

"Yes. Go team indeed. Thank you. Boys, why don't you say goodnight to your uncle and Lee, clean up this mess then get ready for bed?" Lexie waited for the groans to finish before adding, "You can read for an hour before lights out."

The boys doled out hugs goodnight to everyone and Lee was pleasantly surprised to be included.

"Thanks again for helping me figure out my project, Uncle Lee."

"No problem. Anytime."

Lee followed the other adults downstairs to the kitchen so Lexie and Matt could eat. Matt stood at the counter facing them, as Lee, Saul and Lexie each took a seat on the stools at the high breakfast counter.

Lexie groaned in pleasure as she bit into her slice.

"Hungry, Lex?"

"Starving, little brother."

"Uncle Lee, huh? That was fast," Matt said with a chuckle as he snagged his own piece of pizza from the box on the counter.

"I didn't ask them to. They just started calling me that about an hour ago."

"It's not a problem. It means they like you. They never called my sister's husband 'uncle' and they were married for three years before she caught him cheating. They seem to be great judges of character, so welcome to the insanity that is being part of this family."

Lexie reached out to smack Matt on the shoulder. "Quit. You're going to scare him off. We're really not that bad, Lee."

"Yes, we are. Especially when we're all together," Saul disagreed. "But it's all done out of love."

"Yep," Matt continued. "The Valencias would do anything for each other. Once you're Mama-approved, there's no escape. When's she coming again for a visit?"

"Two weeks," Lexie answered her husband. "She and Dad are coming to stay with the boys so I can go to that conference with you in San Diego."

"Oh, that's right. At least my hand should be mostly healed by then and the stitches will be out. We can get some waterproof Band-Aids before we go, so I can go swimming and stuff." Matt raised his bandaged hand and showed it to them to emphasize his point.

"Should I be worried?" Lee had to ask.

"Lee, I think she's going to love you. I haven't seen my dear brother smile this much in forever."

Lee shared a smile with Saul as Saul took his hand where it rested on the counter. They spent the next hour sitting at the breakfast bar just talking.

"Well, I hate to break up the party, but we should go make sure the boys turn out their lights. School and workday tomorrow," Lexie said.

Matt groaned. "Don't remind me. This weekend flew by."

Lexie and Matt escorted Lee and Saul to the door, where Lexie pulled Lee into a hug. "Don't be a stranger. I really would like to get to know you better."

Saul pulled Lee away from his sister before leaning down and kissing her cheek. "You'll have plenty of time. He's not going anywhere."

"Aw. That's so sweet. Can't wait to call Mom. Later." With a wave, Lexie was up the stairs, already pulling out her phone.

Matt chuckled before giving Saul a side hug then shaking Lee's hand. "I guess I'm on bad-cop duty tonight. Nice getting a chance to meet you."

Saul took Lee's hand and walked him to the passenger side, before opening it and waiting for Lee to climb in. "Thank you."

Lee looked up at Saul, startled. "For what?"

"Just for being you." Saul leaned in for a kiss before pulling back with a groan a moment later. "What do you say we take this somewhere more private?"

"Sounds like a plan to me."

Saul closed the door and made his way to the driver's side. "Told you there was nothing to worry about."

"I haven't met your parents yet."

"They'll love you too. You already have the terrible twosome's seal of approval."

"Hope you're right."

Chapter Seven

Saul dropped Lee off to pick up his truck, since they'd agreed that made the most sense. Lee followed Saul as they drove the five miles from the house back to the garage. He was getting nervous for a completely different reason now. Their relationship was finally moving forward, and while he certainly had his fair share of mutual hand jobs and blow jobs under his belt, he had yet to go any further. Trying to fly under the radar at home meant that he had never actually made it to a bed for any of his sexual escapades.

Lee snorted and muttered out loud, "Escapades. I wonder what actually constitutes an *escapade*? Have I ever actually had an escapade? Hey, Siri," Lee asked his phone, "what's the definition of 'escapade'?"

The mechanical voice answered, "An act or incident involving excitement, daring or adventure."

"Okay, so there was a little excitement involved. I wouldn't say there was any daring or adventure, though. Oh God, I'm twenty-two and I've never had an escapade. What if I'm horrible at sex?"

Lee was so busy freaking out that he hadn't even realized they'd made it back to the garage until Saul knocked on his partially opened window. Lee jumped before rolling it down the rest of the way. "You have *got* to stop doing that."

Saul chuckled. "You were a little zoned out. You okay?"

Lee shook his head. "I'm fine. Let me out. I'll open the lot so we're off the street."

After parking and relocking the gate, Saul followed Lee up the stairs to the apartment. Lee had barely stepped inside after unlocking the door before Saul grabbed his arm, swung him around and pressed him against the door. Lee didn't even get a chance for his heart to stop hammering from the scare of being grabbed like that before Saul was kissing him and his heart was pounding for a whole other reason.

Saul kissed him until Lee relaxed into it then Saul said, "Yes, people can be bad at sex. You and I together are pure combustion, though, baby, and there is no way you are going to be horrible. Has somebody told you that you were horrible at sex?" Saul looked completely pissed off at the thought that someone would have said anything like that to him.

Lee gulped, trying to get past the fact that Saul had heard what he'd said to himself. "Truth is, I haven't actually had sex. Hand jobs, blow jobs, yes, but nothing else."

Saul's gaze softened. "We don't have to do —"

Lee interrupted. "I want to. I really, really want to. I just don't want to disappoint you." Lee pressed his lips to Saul's in a desperate rush, not wanting him to change his mind.

Saul grabbed the hair at the back of Lee's head and tugged gently. "Lee, if you're sure, let's move this to the bedroom. Your first time is definitely not going to be against the door of your apartment."

"But we can revisit the idea later?" Lee watched as Saul's eyes dilated to where there was very little color left. Lee shrugged and tried to drop his head, but Saul tangled his hand in Lee's hair and made it impossible. "I like that you want me so much."

Saul groaned as if he were in pain. "Lee. To the bedroom. *Now*. I'll lock up. It will give me a few minutes to calm down. *Go!*"

Lee went. In the bedroom, he stopped at the doorway, not sure what to do. He just stared at the messy unmade bed. *Should I make the bed? Fold down the blankets? Strip naked? Wait for Saul?* He took one step toward the bed before taking one step toward the hamper instead. Saul came in the room just as Lee finally decided to straighten up the bed a little.

Saul chuckled. "Don't worry about the bed, Lee. We're getting ready to mess it up a heck of a lot more. Let's see if we can move this along." Saul then tackled Lee to the bed in a rush.

"Showing off your football skills, big guy?" Lee asked when he stopped laughing.

"Like you are that much smaller than me." Saul brushed Lee's hair back from his face as he spoke. "That's one of the things I like about you. I don't have to worry about breaking you."

Saul leaned down and kissed the smile off Lee's face. Lee moaned as the kiss deepened.

"What do you say to losing the clothes?"

Lee moaned again as he dragged his hands reluctantly from where he'd been running them up and down Saul's back under his shirt, and he reversed direction and pushed the shirt upward. Saul pushed himself to a sitting position, pulling Lee with him as he sat up, before allowing Lee to pull the shirt the rest of the way up and off.

Saul then reached for Lee's shirt and helped him do the same. Saul stood next to the bed and shed his pants and underwear in one swift motion before leaning down to yank off first one then the other sock. Lee could only stare in awe. He'd been so focused on Saul's cock earlier that he hadn't taken the time to realize that the rest of him was just as amazing.

"Oh, wow."

"What?" Saul asked, his gaze snapping to Lee's from where he had been looking at Lee's naked chest.

"You're gorgeous. Everywhere. Just gorgeous."

Saul chuckled, raised his hands and spun in a slow circle. "You like?"

"Oh yeah. Come here."

"Nope. Get naked first."

Lee rolled his eyes at Saul before standing up to strip off his clothing too. "Hope you're not too disappointed. I'm nowhere near as sexy as you." Lee looked up from where he was removing his last sock to find Saul staring at him and Saul didn't seem disappointed at all.

Saul raised his finger and made the spinning motion. Lee mimicked Saul's earlier actions, raising his hands and turning in a slow circle. He heard a guttural groan come from Saul. Lee whipped his head around as Saul walked toward him in a predatory manner. Lee now had a very good idea what prey felt like. He couldn't say he minded it in this instance, though.

Saul drew Lee into his arms and pressed all their various body parts together. What had felt fantastic clothed was life-altering naked.

"What was that?" Saul asked as he leaned back so he could see Lee's face.

Lee moaned as he began to rub his body against Saul a little bit, feeling Saul's chest hair rubbing against his nipples. Lee himself had very little body hair and virtually none on his chest. Not by choice, though. He certainly wasn't the type to wax. He just didn't grow any. "I think I just found Jesus."

That surprised a bark of laughter out of Saul. "Are you saying being with me is a religious experience?"

"Oh yeah."

"Well, let's see if I can introduce you to God then." Saul maneuvered them so they were back on the bed with Lee on the bottom. Before Lee could come up with a snarky reply, Saul started kissing him. When he stopped, Saul said, "Where's your lube, babe?"

Lee felt like all his brain cells had been fried by Saul's kisses. It really wasn't fair for Saul to ask him questions and expect him to answer coherently. He pointed vaguely in the direction of the table on the right side of the bed before a thought snapped him back into focus.

"Oh shit, I don't have any condoms."

Saul paused in his path toward the drawer. "Do we need them? I haven't been with anyone in over a year. I've been tested since."

"As you know, I haven't been with anyone ever. I've always been careful, and I was tested a couple months ago. If we do this, though, it means commitment to me. You know that, right?"

"I'm already committed, babe," Saul said, putting his hand on Lee's cheek. "I've just been waiting for you."

Lee leaned into Saul's touch before raising up and giving him a quick kiss. "Okay. No condoms. Just us."

Saul gave Lee a hug before laying him back down and rummaging through the drawer. A few moments later he triumphantly waved the bottle. Lowering himself back on top of Lee, he dropped the bottle next to Lee's hip.

"We'll go slow."

"You don't have to go that slow. I have toys." Lee stopped talking in embarrassment as he realized what he'd just admitted.

"Really? What kind of toys? Are they in that same drawer?" Saul moved to look but Lee hauled him back.

"Never mind about that. How about you just focus on being my real boyfriend instead of looking for my imaginary one?"

Saul chuckled. "Imaginary boyfriend, huh? Should I be jealous?"

"Well, since I always imagined it was you, probably not," Lee admitted shyly.

Saul groaned. "You're killing me here," he said before diving in for another mind-numbing kiss.

Saul moved his weight to the side a little and started running a hand over Lee's chest, circling his nipples, then lowered it to his straining cock. Lee groaned in frustration when Saul bypassed it and went to his balls, weighing each one in his hand before running his finger up the vein in Lee's cock to the slit. Saul copied Lee's earlier move and captured a drop of pre-cum and raised it to his lips. Saul hummed in obvious appreciation before repeating the path down Lee's body with his lips and tongue this time, instead of his finger. Saul took extra time sucking on Lee's nipples as Lee writhed on the bed.

Saul engulfed the head of Lee's cock in his mouth and slowly lowered until he reached the bottom.

"Holy fuck! Do you *not* have a gag reflex?"

Saul came back up and licked the head of Lee's dick while slowly shaking his head.

"I am the luckiest guy on the whole fucking planet. Don't stop," Lee begged.

Saul chuckled then hummed as he lowered his head again, making Lee twist his hands in the bedsheet to stop himself from grabbing Saul's head and chasing his release. Lee distantly heard the snick of the cap as Saul opened the lube before swallowing his dick back down. A slick finger circled his entrance for a moment, before the questing finger slowly entered him. Lee tried to focus on relaxing so Saul could prep him when Saul moved from one to two then three fingers, but it was hard when any brain cells he had seemed to be offline at the moment.

Lee had to take deep breaths and concentrate on not blowing when Saul rubbed his finger across his prostate. "You need to stop that. I don't want to come until you're inside me."

"You think you're ready?"

"Please." Lee nodded his head before pulling his knees up to his chest.

"It might be easier for your first time if you roll over."

"No. I want to see you. *Please.*"

"Okay. Well, let me at least do this."

Saul took one of the pillows and put it under Lee's hips, raising him to the perfect angle. Taking one of Lee's legs in hand, he raised it to his shoulder, kissing the ankle before pushing the remaining leg out to the side. Lining up his cock, Saul slowly entered Lee.

Lee remembered to push out and barely remembered to breathe, but Saul continued pushing in until his hips met Lee's ass.

"Okay?"

"Just give me a minute."

"Tell me when you're ready. This is at *your* pace." Saul lowered his forehead to Lee's and lightly kissed Lee's lips.

After a few moments, the pressure eased and Lee lifted his hips, indicating that Saul could continue. Saul gave Lee another kiss then started moving, slowly at first before picking up the pace as they got their timing in sync.

Lee ran his hands over wherever he could reach, then focused his attention on Saul's nipples after pulling on them garnered a deep groan and a harder thrust. Crunching up, Lee took Saul's right nipple into his mouth, moaning when the move positioned him, so Saul was pushing on his prostate with every inward stroke. He sucked then lightly bit, causing Saul to push harder.

"There! Right there!" Lee shouted around his mouthful of nipple before switching to the other side. Three more perfect thrusts had Lee throwing himself back and rocking his hips up hard, as his orgasm washed over him. Saul must have been waiting for him, because he followed right after.

Lee enjoyed the feel of Saul's cum spurting inside him. He wrapped Saul in his arms and welcomed the feel of his weight crushing him into the mattress, up until the moment cum started leaking out of his ass.

"Ew-w, that is a weird feeling."

Saul chuckled before slowly sliding out of Lee and lying down next to him. "Give me a minute and I'll go get a cloth to clean us up. I have to be able to feel my legs first, though.

Lee chuckled and leaned down to remove the pillow from under his butt before rolling over and sprawling on Saul's chest.

"And, Lee?" Lee raised his head to look in Saul's eyes. "You weren't horrible at sex." Saul chuckled when Lee dropped his head back down with a thud and smacked him on the pec. "In fact," Saul continued, wrapping his arms around Lee, "if it gets any better, I might not survive."

Lee hid his grin by kissing Saul's nipple, grinning wider when it made Saul shudder. Lee then closed his eyes, burrowed closer and dozed off. He woke to the feel of a warm cloth cleaning him off and groaned as he rolled over onto his back to peer up at Saul.

"Hey. Sorry. Didn't mean to fall asleep," Lee whispered.

Saul whispered back, "Don't worry about it. It's been a rough couple of days for both of us. I dozed off too. Be right back." Saul went to put the washcloth in the hamper before returning and climbing back into bed with Lee, pulling the covers up and over them as he did.

"Get back over here." Saul pulled Lee back into his embrace with Lee's head on his shoulder.

"I'm not too heavy or too hot?"

"Not at all. I like knowing right where you are. I finally have you right where I want you. Get some sleep." Saul ran his hand over the back of Lee's head in a petting motion.

"Good night, Saul."

"Night, babe."

Chapter Eight

Saul woke to the sound of his alarm going off on his phone. Moaning, he rolled over onto his back before reaching to shut off the annoying sound. He paused when he registered the nightstand was a light oak color rather than his own dark-colored one. The day before came back to him in a rush as he turned his head to look for Lee.

"Looking for me?" Lee's voice came from the doorway. He walked to the bed carrying a tray with coffee, eggs and bacon.

"Please tell me the coffee is for me." Saul couldn't do anything about the pleading tone to his voice.

Lee chuckled. "All of it is for you, actually. I already ate. I have to leave in a couple minutes to get to work, but I was warned about making sure you have plenty of coffee in the morning."

Saul arranged the pillows behind him before he took the cup from the tray, inhaled the aroma and took a sip. "Ah-h."

"Should I leave the two of you alone?"

Saul looked to see that Lee had one eyebrow raised in query and a smirk on his lips.

Saul pretended to think about it before reaching out to take Lee's hand and raise it to his lips, then tugging him to sit. Saul leaned back against the pillows and threw his arm over Lee's shoulders. "A perfect start to the day."

"Wouldn't the perfect start to the day be a blow job *then* a cup of coffee?"

"Smartass, but no. Just you and coffee are all it takes to make a perfect start."

Lee flushed. "Sweet talker."

"I love seeing you blush, and I can't wait to find out how far down the blush goes." He ended with a waggle of his eyebrows, making Lee laugh.

"But you won't find out right now. Eat your breakfast. I have to get to work." Lee got up off the bed but Saul grabbed his hand and pulled so he bent down.

"I need a kiss before you go."

Lee leaned in and gave Saul a kiss and a careful hug around the cup of coffee, before standing back up straight and heading to the door, speaking over his shoulder.

"You coming back here after work or did you have something else going on tonight?"

"I'll come back here if that's okay?"

"Of course it's okay. I'll put some steaks in the fridge to defrost and we can grill outside."

"Sounds great." *Perfect start to the day.* Saul dug into his breakfast, alternating between bites of food and sips of coffee, before looking at the clock and realizing he needed to get a move on if he was going to make it to his meeting on time. He jumped into the shower and washed up before getting dressed and grabbing his dishes to take them to the kitchen to load into the dishwasher. Saul was surprised to see that Lee had already washed the pans he'd used for cooking, although he guessed he shouldn't be, with how neat Lee kept everything. He found a travel mug filled with coffee on the counter with a sticky note attached. Saul chuckled as he read what it said.

Anti-grump potion. Drink until gone. Lee.

He'd also doodled an ogre on the bottom. Saul pocketed the note, picked up the coffee cup and headed for his truck. Glancing toward the bay door, he saw Lee looking at him. Saul raised his travel mug in salute and gave him a wave before climbing in his truck and pulling away.

The trip to work passed in a haze of happiness as he thought about the night before and the start to his day. He lowered a hand to his pocket to make sure his drawing treasure was still there. He couldn't wait to hang it on his monitor at work. It would definitely make him smile whenever he saw it. He needed to get a picture of Lee for his desk too.

Shaking his head at his sappiness, he parked his truck in his assigned parking space at the store. Walking toward the new office building for the meeting with the construction supervisor, Saul ran into Eric on the sidewalk. The normally laid-back man looked pissed off and worn.

"What's up? You look like you're ready to kill someone."

"Just had an emergency meeting with the principal at Sam and Claire's school."

"What did the principal have to say?"

"Oh, he said all the right things. He was just as shocked as we were. *'Were we sure? Didn't sound like Mrs. Jackson.'* Etcetera, etcetera. It went south when he pulled Mrs. Jackson into the meeting. That woman is just vile. She started spouting off about Christian values and how the country has just gone downhill and allowing two men to get married is just wrong. The principal looked absolutely shocked, then he told Mrs. Jackson to go to the conference room and wait for him there. After she left, he told us that he had to follow policy as far as disciplining her was concerned, but they were an inclusive school and did not share her opinion, blah, blah, blah. In the meantime, he said he could at least move Sam to a different classroom. Since Claire and Sam live in the same house, they don't normally recommend they be put in the same one, but Kirk and I kind of insisted."

"Yeah, probably a good idea. Those girls are tight, and they have a lot of changes coming up."

"Right?" Eric sighed and rubbed his temples. "The principal didn't want to make a big deal about it, so he asked if they could just have Sam switch classes tomorrow. He said that Mrs. Jackson would not be returning today. I kind of took that to mean she was going to be suspended pending an investigation, but who knows how it works."

"Well, Sam will be happy to be in the same class as Claire. Claire loves her teacher, right?"

"Yeah. Mr. Hines is a great teacher—and very liberal, if the rainbow bumper sticker on his car is any indication."

"Well, that's good."

"Yeah. Kirk and I are debating whether we should put them in a private school, but Kirk wants to give them a chance to make it right. The school does have a great reputation. That's why I was so shocked by this woman. I can't believe I missed it."

Saul stopped and put his hand on Eric's shoulder. "Stop beating yourself up. You fixed it as soon as you found out and Sam and Claire now know to come to you if anyone says anything that upsets them."

"I know. I know. It's just that we were so happy, you know? And this woman has to come along with her prejudices and tried to ruin it."

"Well, she didn't succeed. Now you guys are going to be stronger than ever. You learned some very important lessons. Ironically, the same lesson I learned," Saul said with a grimace. "Communication. Communication is key."

"I hear that. You and Lee work things out?" Eric chuckled at the grin that spread across Saul's face. "I take it yes?"

"Yeah. We're good now." Saul sobered. "I almost blew it, though. I want to make sure I never screw up like that again."

"As you said, communication."

"Yeah." Reaching for the door, Saul opened it then indicated for Eric to go in ahead of him. "Let's get this meeting done."

"Wow," Eric said as they walked into the totally renovated space, "this looks amazing."

"It really does."

"Glad you think so." A voice came from the doorway which led into the break area.

"Jonah, good to see you, man." Saul walked forward and offered their contractor his hand. "You've done a great job here."

"Thanks. You should see what we've done upstairs. I'm just doing the final touch-ups on the paint here and we are about two days out from finishing the apartment. Inspections are scheduled for the end of the week. We're hoping to have the certificate of occupancy for you then. Have a look around down here while I finish this last thing in the breakroom then we can go upstairs together."

"Sounds good," Eric said, stepping up and shaking Jonah's hand as well. "It looks so different from the outdated mess it was before."

"Yeah," Saul agreed. "Big improvement. It looks huge without all the construction equipment in here too," Saul added.

"I'm sure that will change once we get all the workstations in. It's still a great space, though. I'll call our designer and give her a heads-up that it will probably be a 'go' by the end of the week. "

"Debbie will be so excited."

Eric chuckled. "She has been chomping at the bit to get started, hasn't she?"

"She has indeed." Saul peeked into what would be his new office before glancing into Eric's then checking out the restrooms. "It all looks great, Jonah."

"Thanks. Let's head upstairs and check it out. I think you'll really like what we've done. This is the internal door. It has a separate punch-code keypad with battery backup being installed so people can't get in unless you give them the access code. You have another entrance around back, which will have the same system, as well as the garage. As requested, there are two separate security systems, so you don't have to disarm the office when you come in and out of your personal space."

The three men filed up the stairs to the apartment. The door at the top of the stairs entered into the kitchen. All of the stainless-steel appliances and granite gleamed.

"Saul, this looks amazing. Look at all the counters! You can seat, what?" He paused, obviously trying to figure out the number. "Five at the breakfast bar?"

"Six, actually," Jonah answered.

"Wow. I'm totally jealous. This open floor plan is amazing too. Look at all those windows." Eric stepped up and looked out of the windows in the living area, which had a view into the courtyard between the buildings.

"I know, right? It lets in a ton of light and I splurged and got the privacy windows that let me see out but people can't see in, so I don't have to worry about having to keep curtains or blinds closed all the time."

"Certainly worth it."

Saul grinned. "I'm very happy with it. The space certainly feels like me."

"I can't wait to see it finished."

"I can't wait either. What's left, Jonah?"

"We finally got in the tiles for the master bath shower. Those have to be installed and grouted then the fixtures installed once everything is set. Those are the major things. The rest are just touch-ups, at this point."

Saul and Eric wandered through the rest of the large apartment.

"Has Lee seen it yet?"

"Nope. He helped me pick out the tile for the master bath, but he hasn't been in the space. I can't wait to show him."

"You going to get him to help you look for stuff for it?"

"Yeah. Since I plan on talking him into moving in here with me, sooner rather than later, it's probably a good idea."

Eric laughed. "Does Lee know he's moving in with you?"

Saul looked back at Eric without a trace of humor on his face. "I told him I wasn't letting him go, Eric. He's it for me."

A huge smile spread across Eric's face. "Yeah?" At Saul's nod, Eric slapped him on the back and gave him a side-arm hug. "Being in love looks good on you, man."

"Being in love feels good too."

"When does he meet Mama V then?"

"She comes in two weeks. I was thinking we should start with a Skype call, though, or Lee will stress himself out completely between now and then."

"Good idea. I swear that if worrying were an Olympic sport, he'd win gold."

"Right?" Saul paused a moment. "I wouldn't have him any other way, though. It's part of what makes him Lee. I just want to be his safe place."

"Man, when did we become so sappy?"

"When we met the guys who made it necessary?"

"Oh yeah, that would do it."

Chapter Nine

Lee went to lock the gate to the back lot now that the rest of the employees had left for the day. Saul had left from his work an hour or so earlier to pick his parents up at the airport. Even though Lee had spoken to them via Skype several times at this point, he was still a nervous wreck about meeting them. Saul was going to swing by and get him after picking them up before they all went to Lexie's for dinner.

The original plan had been for them to go to the airport together, but Murphy's Law had been a bitch at the garage. Nothing had gone right, starting with the front desk computer refusing to boot up, and they'd run behind all day. Saul was giving Lee a chance to shower and change, since one of the issues was a brake line bursting and spraying brake fluid everywhere. Lee still felt absolutely gross, even after he'd taken a quick shower and put clean clothes on right after it had happened. He was definitely looking forward to another hot shower now that the workday was finally over.

A noise to his left had him turning his head to investigate. He froze when he saw his brother standing there.

"Hey, little brother," Frank said with a sneer.

Lee made sure to stand up straight and look his brother in the eye. He was done being afraid. He was surprised when he did so that he was three or four inches taller than his brother. *Broader too. Huh. When did that happen? It's amazing what you notice when you take your eyes off the ground.* Lee saw the exact moment his brother realized it too, because he took a step back and the sneer fell from his face. Frank seemed to hate himself for it, though, because a moment later the sneer was back and he puffed up.

Lee raised an eyebrow. "What do you want?"

"You need to come back to work with me and Dad."

"And why would I do that? I'm happy here."

"Sergei Barinov saw the work you did for Stuart and came to ask us to do something for him. I told him we could."

"And what does that have to do with me?"

"It's big money. He gave a huge deposit. We have to come through for him."

"You need to give his money back then, because I'm not coming back to work for you and Dad. You obviously know where I'm working. Tell him where I am and be done with it." Lee saw a strange expression cross Frank's face. An ugly suspicion sprouted in his mind. "You already spent the money, didn't you? You took a deposit from a suspected member of the local Russian Mob for work you couldn't do and you spent it. You're a moron."

Frank rushed Lee and shoved him back against the chain-link fence, grabbing a handful of the front of

Lee's uniform shirt in the process. Frank yanked Lee down so they were eye-to-eye. "You *will* come back and do this job, or I'll leak it to the press about Saul Valencia being a rotten faggot. I saw the two of you. I have pictures on my phone. He had his tongue down your throat. You disgust me, but I'm sure someone will pay me big money for the story."

Lee froze, in confusion more than anything. "Have you been following me? Wait! Are you trying to *blackmail* me?"

"Whatever works. You will save my ass by doing this job and you'll do whatever else I ask of you without question or I *will* go to the press. Imagine what that could do to the great Saul Valencia's business. Do what I say. Understand?" Then Frank hauled back and punched Lee in the stomach, making him double over in pain—or he would have if Frank didn't still have hold of his shirt front.

"Now, I'll leave you to think about your answer. If I don't see you in a week, I go to the press. You're going to save me one way or another, little brother." Frank then shoved Lee away before stalking off, turning at the corner to glare at Lee one more time.

Lee collapsed onto the ground, clutching his stomach. He really should have expected the punch, but he'd just been so surprised by what Frank had been saying. Lee worked on breathing through his nose and out through his mouth to combat the nausea. He really didn't want to puke. He distantly heard a car pull up, then Saul was there a moment later.

"Lee, are you okay?"

Looking up and seeing Saul's troubled face was bad enough, but over Saul's shoulder, Lee could see Saul's mom and dad still standing next to the car, also staring at him with concern.

"Great way for me to meet your folks," Lee muttered, before making the attempt to stand back up. Saul offered his hand and hauled him to his feet.

"What happened?" Saul asked while looking around.

"Frank. Frank happened."

"Your brother? Did he hit you?"

"Yeah."

"Why would your brother track you down and punch you? That makes no sense."

"It's a long story."

"Perhaps we should take him up to his apartment and get him off the street. Eh, my son?" Saul's mother's slightly accented voice came from just behind Saul. Lee hadn't noticed them move closer behind Saul's bulk and he jumped in reaction.

Saul pulled Lee into his arms and rubbed his back. "Are you hurt anywhere? Can you walk okay?"

"My pride is hurt more than anything. He just punched me in the stomach and knocked the wind out of me is all."

"Okay then, let's do as Mama says and go up to your apartment."

Lee led the way up the back stairs to the apartment after making sure the gate was locked behind them. He didn't think his brother would come back right away, but better to be safe than sorry. Saul's hand in his was a definite comfort. He wasn't used to having someone worried about him, not since his mom had died, at any rate.

Lee unlocked the door and made his way to the couch to sit down. "Please have a seat, Mr. and Mrs. Valencia. I'm sorry for the drama."

"I do not think it is you who has made the drama, young man." Saul's mom came to sit next to Lee on the couch as she spoke. Lee just looked at her in surprise. She took his face in her hands and stared into his eyes for a moment, seeming to peer into his very soul. A wave of some unidentifiable emotion passed through Lee as she looked. "You look like a man who needs to be loved and loved hard. You and Saul will do well for each other. Saul has told me your mama has died, no?"

"Yes. She died eight, almost nine years ago."

"While I cannot replace her, I can love you as a mama does. Please, call me Mama. Saul says he is keeping you, so we may as well start as we mean to go on."

Lee swallowed hard, trying to keep the emotion contained. "Why?" he asked in a whisper. "You don't know me. We've only talked on the phone or Skyped a couple of times."

"Saul has told me much about you over these last few months." Obviously seeing his surprise, she cupped his chin in her hand, making sure he made eye contact and she explained. "Yes, even though you and I did not talk until recently, I talked to my son every day. He told me of you, and I heard in his voice how much he cared. I waited until he was ready to introduce us. You are the first to be deemed worthy to meet us, the first to pass the Lexie test. That tells me how he feels for you. My Saul, he talks a lot, but you have to learn to listen to hear his heart. He has kept it safe…until you."

That last bit, along with the look of understanding and affection, was what broke Lee and he could no longer swallow the emotions he'd kept bottled for so long. He choked on a sob. Mama simply pulled Lee into her embrace and petted his hair as he finally let it all go. Once the sobs trickled down to an occasional sniff, she gave him a kiss on the top of the head before easing him away from her and into Saul's arms.

"There. That is better, no?" she asked as she continued to rub her hand up and down his back.

Lee could only nod from where he had his head buried in the space between Saul's neck and shoulder. "I'm sorry."

"What is it you are sorry for?"

"The drama."

"And as I said, I don't think it is you who brought the drama. Why don't you go shower and change your clothes? I will call Lexie and let her know we will be a little later than planned."

Saul gave Lee another hug then pushed him back so he could give him a soft kiss. "Let's get you in the shower. I'll grab you some clothes and meet you there. Okay?"

"Yeah," Lee answered, giving him another quick hug before standing and making his way to the bathroom. Once there, he stood and stared at himself in the mirror. He looked wrecked. He had dirt on him from where he'd been on the ground. Tear tracks stained his face. Turning his head, he saw that he had a bit of oil behind his ear. "Wow, what a great way to make a first impression." Lee could only shake his head.

Saul's voice from the doorway made him jump. "Let me in."

Stepping aside, Lee opened the door and let Saul into the bathroom with him. Saul set the stack of clothes in his arms on the counter, shutting the door with his foot at the same time before pulling Lee into his arms and kissing the side of his head. "You okay?"

"At the moment? Not even close, but I think I will be. We have to talk about what Frank wanted."

"After your shower. It can keep a few more minutes. Get clean." Saul pushed Lee back a little bit so he could look Lee in the eyes. "I love you. No matter what it is, we'll figure it out together. Okay?"

Lee felt more tears flood his eyes and could only nod. Clearing his throat a couple of times, he finally choked out, "I love you too." Saul's face lit up with joy and he wiped Lee's tears with his thumbs before pulling him in for a kiss.

"Get in the shower. We'll be waiting for you when you're done."

Saul then gave him one more kiss and a shove in the direction of the shower before letting himself out of the bathroom. Lee was mindful of people waiting for him and tried to hurry, while also trying to be thorough. Climbing out of the shower and grabbing a towel, he glanced down to see a bruise already starting to form where his brother had punched him. He trailed his fingers over the mark for a moment before reaching for his deodorant, putting it on and brushing his teeth and hair. After pulling on his clothes, Lee looked at himself critically in the mirror. His eyes were still red-rimmed from crying, but he was clean. *Going to have to deal with all this.*

Lee exited the bathroom to the sound of a discussion between Saul and his mother.

"He has no food in his apartment."

"Lee doesn't cook, Mama," Saul answered, the amusement clear in his tone. "He can make breakfast and he can grill, but that is the extent of his cooking abilities. He can't be good at everything. If he was any more perfect, he wouldn't want my sorry ass."

"Hmph. Don't curse."

Lee made eye contact with Saul's father as he rounded the corner and they both grinned. "Well, you look better, son."

"I feel a bit better. Thank you all for being patient with me."

"It's what family does." Saul's father said it so casually, as if all of this acceptance wasn't life-altering for Lee. "Now, let's head over to Lexie's. She has dinner just about ready, and I, for one, am starved. We can discuss whatever is going on afterward. Everything feels better on a full stomach." Then he clapped his hand on Lee's shoulder and gave it a squeeze before heading for the door, collecting his wife as he went by. "Come along, Mama."

"How can he have no food?"

Saul chuckled before coming over to take Lee's hand. "Come on. Let's catch up with them. Expect a lecture about your lack of groceries on the ride, though."

"Got it."

Lee was glad Saul had warned him, because the ride over did indeed include a gentle lecture from Saul's mother about his lack of food options in his cupboards. Lee couldn't stop grinning, though, since it was so nice to have a mother worrying over him once more.

Dinner at Lexie's was just what Lee needed. Laughter and chaos. The boys and dogs had greeted everyone in their typical exuberant manner. Dinner had involved lots of food and conversation.

"Hey, Nick, how did your science fair presentation go?" Lee asked as Lexie went to grab dessert.

"It went awesome. Thanks again for your help. It definitely wasn't boring." Nick made a face as he said the word 'boring'.

"Why was this important to not be boring?" Mama asked with an arched brow.

Andy was the one to jump in and answer, as Nick blushed. "Ashley told him that she was sure his presentation would be another snoozefest and she wasn't looking forward to it."

"Who is this Ashley girl?" Mama's outrage was even greater than that over Lee's empty pantry, and he had to stifle a chuckle.

"Mama," Lexie interjected, "it's all good now. They're actually dating."

"No, we're not."

"You're *not*?" Lexie turned to her son in confusion.

"Nope. We broke up."

"Why?"

"I didn't notice she got her hair cut." Nick shrugged as he answered. "It looked exactly the same."

Lee lost the battle of trying to contain his amusement and he laughed out loud. As he wasn't the only one, he didn't feel bad about it.

After dessert, the boys were sent up to the bonus room while the adults had the beverage of their choice sitting at the table. For Lee, it was a Coke. For the others, it was coffee.

"Now," Mama began after the boys were gone, "let's discuss what it is your brother wanted with you. Saul told me your father and brother threw you away for being gay." Lee nodded since she seemed to be waiting for some kind of response. "Then they do not know the meaning of family. Family loves and cares for one another, no matter what. That one who would hit you? He is not family. *We* will now be your family."

"But you don't even know what he wanted, what he said."

"So, tell us. Tell us why this man would think it okay to punch you and hurt you."

Saul scooted his chair closer and took Lee's hand in his. Lee gave Saul's hand a squeeze before taking a deep breath and starting. "Sergei Barinov somehow saw the paint job I did on this guy's motorcycle." Turning to Saul he said, "You remember Stuart, right?"

"The guy we met at dinner one night who wanted to date you," Saul answered with a growl. The possessiveness made Lee shiver, even as he laughed at him.

"Yeah. The guy who I didn't even notice was hitting on me because I only have eyes for you." With an eyeroll, he turned back to everyone else and continued, "Anyway, Sergei went to my dad's place to get something done for his own motorcycle. Frank took a deposit toward the work and he has spent it."

Saul's sucked-in breath indicated he knew what that meant, but everyone else just looked confused.

"Sergei Barinov is part of the Russian immigrant population around here—rumored to be Russian Mafia."

"Wait! Barinov... Wasn't he the boy who was on your team at college? The one you had a crush on, but who had a girlfriend?" Lexie asked with a snicker.

"His name *was* Barinov, but not Sergei. His name was Alexis."

"That story was about Alexis Barinov? You had a crush on *Alexis*?" Lee started laughing.

"What's so funny about that?"

"I lived in the same neighborhood as Alexis' family. I went to school with his half-brother, Dimitri. Even though he was so much older than us, his brother talked about him like he was a god. The way he tells it,

Alexis slept with the entire cheerleading squad in high school."

"Well, I am glad your tastes have improved." Mama sniffed to show her obvious disdain for Saul's previous choices. "Is he related to this Sergei?"

"I think he is his nephew or cousin or something, but they aren't close," Lee answered. "I've heard Sergei is close with a couple of his other cousins, but not Alexis or his siblings. I've never seen Sergei in the neighborhood, at any rate."

"What does your brother spending the deposit have to do with you?" Lexie asked after getting her snickers under control.

"He wants me to come back and work for him and Dad again and do the work. I told him no, that I was happy where I was and to send Sergei to me if they couldn't do the work. He said if I didn't do it, he was going to get the money one way or another by selling pictures to the paparazzi of Saul and I kissing. Well, he said to 'the papers', but…" Lee ended in a shrug. "He said that it would ruin Saul and his business."

Saul barked out a laugh as everyone spoke at once, condemning Frank.

"He won't ruin my business. Lee. V & H has a great reputation for having quality products at good prices. Even if we take a short-term hit, I'm sure we'll be fine. Let me call Eric and Kirk and get them over here. They should be involved in the plan for how we're going to attack this, since it affects them too."

"It would probably be easier if I just went back and did the job," Lee said with a sigh, hanging his head.

"Lee… Babe…" Saul made Lee look at him. "We have to take a stand now. You know that, right? If we don't,

Frank will continue to pressure you to do things you don't want to do. Right?"

"I know. It just seems like a lot of pressure to put on everyone else. It could affect the garage. It could affect your stores. That's a lot of people to impact."

"But if we cave to him, it means he wins. He doesn't get to win at anything that involves you anymore. Got it?"

Lee nodded, awed again by the love and support he got from this man. His dream. His Saul. Lee gave him a quick kiss before turning toward the now-silent group. "What do we do now?"

"Let me call Kirk and Eric, as I said. They should be involved in the discussion. You call Will."

"Why Will?"

"Because he knows your dad and brother too and, more importantly, he is a vital part of your support system."

Lee thought for a moment before nodding in agreement and pulling out his phone to call Will.

It took less than thirty minutes for everyone to show up and be sitting around the table. The girls were happily upstairs watching a movie with the boys in the bonus room.

"What's going on?" Will was the first to ask, once everyone was settled.

Saul gave a concise explanation of the events leading to the need for the meeting.

"That asshole," Kirk shouted and pounded his fist on the table, making Lee jump. "Thinking he can come in and threaten one of us. He's lucky we weren't there at the time."

"I think that was probably on purpose, Kirk," Eric said dryly. "What are we going to do?"

"*We*? What do you mean 'we'?" Lee asked, confused.

Eric rolled his eyes at Lee, while Will slapped Lee on the back of the head. Lee turned his head and stared at Will.

"What did you do that for?"

"Because you're a dumbass. Of course *we*. We're a family—some by blood, some by choice but family. Family sticks together."

Lee looked around the table and saw a mix of expressions from affection or raised eyebrows from most and a mouthed 'dumbass' from Kirk before he winked at him. A smile pulled at Lee's lips. "Okay. Saul? What are *we* going to do?"

"I think the first step is to call my agent and see if she can get me an interview with someone for me to come out." Everyone just stared at Saul after his announcement.

Eric was the first to recover. "You sure that's what you want to do?"

Saul shrugged. "I'm tired of this being a cloud over me. I'm ready to put it out there on my terms. Of course, I would like it if you were there with me when I did it." Saul squeezed Lee's hand where it rested on the table. "What do you think?"

"I think it sounds absolutely terrifying." Lee swallowed hard. "But if you want me there with you, I'll be there."

A cheer went up at the table.

"I want to be there too," Eric said after the noise had died down. "What do you think, Kirk? It will probably affect you the most. You have a small business."

Kirk took a moment, obviously thinking hard, staring at where he drew designs on the table with his finger. With a decisive nod, he looked first at Eric then at Saul and Lee. "I'm in. It's time to take a stand. Nothing we do is wrong. I'm tired of people acting like I should be ashamed of who I am. I'm proud of who I am as a man and lucky to have found the love of my life. Gay is just a part of what makes me me."

Eric leaned over and gave Kirk a kiss on the cheek. "I'm proud of who you are too, babe, who we are together. We've got your back, Saul."

Mama spoke up next. "Decision made then. Lexie and I will call your other sisters to tell them. Saul, you call your agent and come up with a plan of how to do this."

"Remember, Frank only gave me a week to come do the work or he was going to tell someone," Lee added.

"That means we have to be quick," Eric agreed, pulling out his phone.

Chapter Ten

Saul couldn't believe he was actually doing it. He stared at his agent's number on his phone, frozen with his thumb over the call button. He'd thought about coming out many times. His family had known, of course. He had told his parents and his sisters while he'd been in college. He just couldn't lie to his mama about dating girls while he was away. In high school, he'd hung with a pack of boys and had been very busy with different sports. He legitimately hadn't had time to date.

He'd suppressed his desire for the male of the species and focused on sports. It had just seemed easier. Once he made it to college, he'd fully accepted being gay and he'd become a bit of a slut, but it had never really made him happy. Seeing Eric and Elizabeth together had made Saul realize the reason. He wanted to be in a relationship.

The problem was that he was in the closet. It was hard to be in a relationship from the closet, but he'd had to be if he wanted to play the sport he loved. Homophobia was real and dangerous. Even as big as he was, he'd been afraid. He wasn't playing the sport anymore, though, having retired at thirty-one. His body just couldn't hold up anymore. It had been a relief to lose the extra weight he'd had to pack on to play. He had plenty of money in the bank and a great business with Eric. It was time for the younger guys to have their shot.

He hadn't lied to Lee. He hadn't made a secret of the fact that he was gay since he'd retired, but he hadn't made any announcements. He really didn't think it should matter who he loved. Now, it was time to stand up. He refused to let Lee's brother blackmail him or influence his life in any way if he could help it. He had other dreams he wanted to pursue and most of them revolved around the man currently sitting to his right.

Saul leaned over and kissed Lee's cheek.

"What was that for?"

"I love you."

A huge smile spread across Lee's face. "I love you too." Lee leaned forward and kissed him.

Mama clearing her throat interrupted a very fine kiss. "Boys, we do not have time for the hanky or the panky right now. Saul, call your agent."

"Yes, Mama." Saul chuckled softly at the blush that rose up Lee's face. He did so love to see Lee blush.

He pressed Call on the phone, listening to it ring as he looked around the table. Eric was on the phone with their lawyer. Mama was talking to one of his sisters, while Lexie was talking to another. Matt and Dad were having a quiet conversation that he couldn't hear. Kirk, Will and Lee were talking about adding more security cameras at the garage.

"Saul! To what do I owe this pleasure? I haven't heard from you in a while." The voice of his agent came over the line, settling something in him when he heard her usual brash Jersey accent.

"It's been two weeks, Gracie. Two. Weeks."

"Is that all? Feels like forever. You know you were always my favorite."

"And I also know you tell all your clients that."

"True, but I only mean it with you." Gracie ended with a cackle.

Saul rolled his eyes, even though she couldn't see him. Lord, he loved the woman. She had fought hard for him during every step of his career, from the moment he'd first signed with her. She was a tough agent, well respected and feared in equal measure. If she liked you, she would do anything for you. Saul was lucky she had always liked him. From the first meeting, they had just clicked.

"What can I do for you, Saul? I know you're not calling because you missed my jokes."

"I need your help."

"Anything."

"You don't know what it is yet." Saul chuckled.

"You need an untraceable vat of lye and a shovel? Do we have a body to dispose of?"

"Should I be scared that's where your brain went? Have you had to do that for any of your clients before?" Saul was a little appalled at the possibility.

"Client-agent confidentiality, Sauly. My lips are sealed." Grace paused for a moment before howling with laughter. "Oh, I needed that. Thanks, Saul. Now, seriously, what do you need?"

"I'm gay."

"And?"

"You knew?"

"Of course I knew. What am I, blind? You think I didn't know the reason you were hanging out with that loser David. It wasn't for his brains, that was for sure."

Saul couldn't help but chuckle. "I wish I could argue with you, but he wasn't that bright. He had other good qualities, though."

"Yeah, he must have been amazing in the sack, because you sure couldn't have had many meaningful conversations with him. Wait. Are you wanting to come out?"

"Yeah. I am."

"And is there a reason for this?" Her voice had taken on a wheedling tone.

"Several. The main one being I've met someone."

"I'll be on the first plane out in the morning. I need to meet him."

"He's already got Mama's approval. You're going to love him, but there's more."

Gracie sighed over the phone. "Of course there's more. There always is with you. Give me the short version."

As Saul couldn't deny it, he just continued his explanation. "Short version. My boyfriend's name is Lee Clark. He's absolutely the best thing that has ever happened to me. Twenty-two." Lee tapped him on the shoulder. "Hold on a minute, Gracie." Saul put the phone to his chest and turned to Lee.

"I'm twenty-three."

"What? Since when?"

"Last week."

Saul gave Lee a glare, shocked that he hadn't known and mad that Lee hadn't said anything. "We will talk about this when I'm off the phone." Saul put the phone back to his ear. "Sorry, Gracie. Lee is twenty-three, as he just had a birthday. He's a great mechanic, from what everyone tells me, and an artist with amazing talent. He has painted some custom work on motorcycles as well as some murals for Eric and me.

"He had to leave his father's garage where he'd worked since he was sixteen because his dad and brother found out he was gay. The brother accepted a commission from a dangerous man to do custom paintwork on his bike and is trying to blackmail Lee into doing it or he will out me to the press. I want to get ahead of it."

"And does rat bastard have a name?" Saul could hear Gracie's fingers flying over the keyboard as they talked.

"Frank Clark. Father is Robert Clark, owner of Clark and Sons Garage."

"That gives me a place to start. I'm booked on the six a.m. flight out of Newark. I'll be in Raleigh at eight. Be there to pick me up. Make sure you have coffee." Gracie hung up.

Saul clicked the End button on his phone to see everyone staring at him, waiting to hear the results of the conversation. "She'll be here tomorrow at eight a.m. I'm to pick her up at the airport and bring coffee."

"I can't wait to see her again," Eric stated. "I love that woman. She scares me to death, but I love that woman."

Saul's dad chuckled. "She is indeed a scary one, but she is amazing at her job and she has always done well by Saul."

"I do not know what you are talking about," Mama said with a sniff. "I have always found her simply lovely."

Lee looked at Saul questioningly.

"Gracie is a force of nature. You'll see when you meet her. Don't worry. She's going to love you," Saul said.

"You keep saying that to me."

"And have I been wrong yet?" Saul pulled Lee into his side and gave him a kiss on the temple. "Now, what's this about you having a birthday last week and not telling anyone?"

"What does it matter? It's just a day."

Mama squawked before jumping up and running around the table to pull Lee into a hug. "Birthdays are not just a day, young man. In this family, we celebrate. Now what is the exact day, so none of us will forget again?" Mama gave Saul a look indicating he was now on her list and had some work to do to get off of it.

"My birthday is on the twenty-sixth of October, but really, it's no big deal. No one has celebrated it since before my mom died."

"Now you have people who love and care for you and we *will* celebrate you."

"Just nod and say 'Yes, Mama'," Lexie said. "She's going to get her way anyway, so you might as well just concede now. Save your energy for other things, like the fight ahead."

Lee followed direction and said simply, "Yes, Mama."

"Good boy. You are trainable. That is a good thing in a son-in-law."

"Son-in-law?" It was Lee's turn to squawk.

Saul chuckled. "You're rushing things, Mama. One step at a time. You're overwhelming him."

"Subject change," Kirk interrupted, to Saul's relief. "We'll handle things at the shop tomorrow. I know it's your Saturday to work, Lee, but you need to be with Saul. Will has agreed to fill in for you."

"I didn't have anything planned this weekend. You can make it up to me some other time," Will added.

Lee nodded his agreement.

Eric was next. "I texted Jeff."

"Our lawyer," Saul explained to those who didn't know.

"Yeah. Our lawyer. He will meet us at the new conference room at nine a.m. tomorrow."

"It is good we will have all angles covered," Mama praised. "We have spoken to your sisters to let them know what is coming. They are all behind you one hundred percent. They each said to let them know if they have to come up here."

Saul swallowed hard, overwhelmed. "Thank you, everyone. I appreciate the support more than I can say. Lexie, I know you guys leave for your conference Sunday. We'll keep you posted."

Lexie looked at him as though he had absolutely lost his mind. "I can't go now. I have to stay."

"Lexie, nothing is going to happen immediately. You are only planning on being gone until Wednesday." Saul raised his hand to forestall the coming argument. "I know you've been looking forward to seeing San Diego, and I also know Matt *has* to attend this conference since he's presenting a paper. You can sit in on the meetings tomorrow if you want, but I can almost guarantee nothing is going to happen before Wednesday. It'll take time to get things organized. We'll keep you posted."

Lexie partially gave in with a huff. "We'll see what happens tomorrow then decide."

The meeting broke up shortly afterward with Saul's mother and father settling into the guest room at Lexie and Matt's. One of the items on the agenda for the next day was to show them the surprise of the purchase of Eric's house for them. They had to get through the meeting first, though.

"Come on, babe." Saul took Lee's hand as they walked to his car. "Let's go grab some clothes and stuff for you and head home."

Lee nodded. "I like the way your new place turned out."

"Well, I'm hoping it will soon be *our* place, so I'm glad you like it."

"*Our* place?"

"We said I love you to one another. That means something to me. I personally think people who love each other should be in the same place at night."

"Don't you think we're moving a little fast? We've only been sleeping together for two weeks, dating for eight."

"This is actually slow in my family. When we Valencias meet the one, we know. Mama and Papa married after a week."

"A week? That's fast."

"Yep. Lexie and Matt started living together after a month."

"Wow. And you're sure I'm your one?" Lee's voice trembled with uncertainty.

Saul stopped and turned to face Lee, cupping his face in both hands and staring into his eyes. "I'm *very* sure. I knew from our first date that you were going to be everything to me." Saul gave him a light kiss before pulling away. "Let's continue this discussion at home — and don't think I've forgotten we also need to discuss why you didn't mention your birthday."

Lee's sigh was very young and put upon, for once acting his age. Saul couldn't help but laugh. "What?" Lee barked as he stomped to the car.

"Nothing, love. Let's go home. I want to hold you while we talk."

They had both been quiet on the car ride, first to Lee's apartment to get him some clothes for the next few days then on to Saul's. Once the designer had gotten the go-ahead, she had been a whirlwind, having Saul all moved in within the week. Saul loved everything about his new place, from the big comfortable sectional couch to the special-ordered recliner that was big enough for him to stretch out in. The huge king-sized bed was a particular favorite, especially when he had Lee join him there.

Lee threw his bag into the bedroom while Saul grabbed them each a bottle of water. He placed the bottles on the antique trunk that pulled double duty as a throw holder and coffee table, before sitting with his back in the corner of the couch and his legs spread out along its length, waiting for Lee to come take his place sitting between them.

All was right in his world when Lee was seated in front of him, leaning back against his chest. Saul wrapped his arms around Lee and leaned his head against Lee's where it rested on his shoulder. Contentment crept in and he had to struggle to focus so they could have the discussions he knew they needed to have.

"What should we talk about first?" Saul murmured in Lee's ear. "We're going to skip talking about the situation with your brother and coming out. That's tomorrow's fight."

"I guess let's start with the birthday thing. I really don't see what the big deal is about it. It was a Saturday. I was off. I got to spend it with you. There wasn't anything that would have made that day better."

"A cake? A party? Me telling you 'happy birthday'? None of those would have made it better?"

"Maybe the 'happy birthday' thing, but I don't really like cake."

"You don't like cake?" Saul played up his shock to get a laugh out of Lee. Saul counted it a win when it worked, and Lee relaxed further into his embrace.

"You know I'm not a huge sweets eater. I'm more about the salty. Now if you had gotten me birthday French fries, I would have been a happy camper."

"I'll keep that in mind for next year." Saul sobered. "I guess I'm partly to blame. Like a moron, I never even thought to ask you when your birthday was. I guess I assumed — wrongly, it turns out — that you would tell me when it was getting close."

"Well, you know what happens when you assume," Lee joked with a chuckle.

"Yep. Won't happen again." Saul tightened his arms around Lee and kissed the side of his head. "Now, when can you move in?"

"You were serious about that?"

"Of course I was serious about that. I want you with me. Every night."

"I want that too," Lee whispered.

"Then let's make it happen. Your commute will be a little longer."

Lee chuckled. "Yeah, but I'll get to go to sleep with you every night, so I guess it evens out."

"You guess? You *guess*?" Saul started to tickle Lee until he yelled.

"All right. All right. It more than evens out. Happy?"

"Very." Saul then pulled Lee's head back to deliver a kiss. With no one there to interrupt, it quickly became heated with Lee spinning to straddle Saul's legs so he could get a better angle.

"How about we take this to the bedroom?"

"Sounds like a plan." Lee gasped while doing a slow grind against Saul and taking his mouth in another kiss.

Several more minutes went by before Saul pulled his head back again and stilled Lee's hips. "We need to stop or I'm going to come in my pants. Let's move this to the bedroom."

Lee climbed off Saul's lap with a moan, before holding out his hand to help Saul up. "Come on, old man. I think you need your sleep."

"I'll show you 'old man'." Saul stood and threw Lee over his shoulder like a sack of potatoes, slapping his ass when Lee just laughed. After carrying him into the bedroom, Saul threw Lee onto the bed, watching him bounce. Lee's subsequent laughter made him oh so happy.

Once he'd gotten his giggles under control, Lee sat up and stripped off his shirt, throwing it in the direction of the hamper. "I should insult you more often. I like this caveman side of you."

"You liked that, huh? How about this?" Saul then grabbed Lee by the ankles and pulled him to the edge of the bed where he could have access to the button of his jeans. Undoing it, he then grabbed Lee's pant legs at the cuffs and stripped them off, making Lee's bottom half-bounce on the bed.

Lee just laughed and gave him such a look of adoration that Saul had to pause to hold onto the moment.

"What?" Lee asked with a smirk.

"You are so beautiful."

Lee rolled his eyes at him. "Men aren't beautiful."

"Not true." Saul quickly stripped. "I find you absolutely stunning, inside and out, and I'm so lucky and thankful that you came into my life."

"I'm the lucky one," Lee responded, before shucking off his boxers, scooting up so his head was on one of the pillows then holding out his arms. "I need to hold you and feel you pressing me down into the mattress, please. I don't even care if we do anything else."

Saul couldn't refuse such a heartfelt request and crawled onto the bed then knee-walked until he was over Lee. Saul held Lee's gaze as he lowered his weight onto him and Lee closed strong arms around him. He exhaled as he dropped his head to Lee's shoulder and inhaled Lee's clean, masculine scent.

"I love you. Thank you for giving me a chance and agreeing to move in with me."

"It's not exactly a sacrifice, babe. This apartment is amazing. I'll get to sleep with you every night and, as an added bonus, I'll have you to cook for me, since the way I eat seems to be horrible, according to your mama."

"*Your* mama now too." Saul couldn't help the grin that spread across his face, thinking about the lecture Mama had given Lee on the entire ride over to Lexie's house. "She has adopted you."

Lee paused for a moment. "Let's make a pact not to discuss your mama when we're lying in bed." Lee shuddered beneath him.

"You're the one who brought her up," he reminded.

"I know, but it just feels wrong somehow." Another full body shudder went through Lee, making Saul laugh.

"Well, let's see what I can do to distract you." Saul raised his head and gave Lee a heated kiss. He repositioned himself over Lee and slowly started to grind his cock over Lee's, which had softened somewhat during their discussion but hardened more with every rock of Saul's hips. Their combined pre-cum made the glide easier and easier as they continued to rub against each other.

"Wh-what do you want t-to d-do tonight?" Lee stuttered out the question between kisses.

"This. I want to feel you and breathe you in. It's been a long day and we have an early start tomorrow, but I need to feel you wanting me, loving me."

"Always." Lee gasped the word out as he came. Saul slid in the warm slickness for a half-dozen more thrusts before he joined Lee in climax.

Chapter Eleven

Lee woke to the sound of Saul's alarm going off before snuggling back into Saul's warmth. Lee blearily thought it was a good thing that one of them had remembered to set it. Lee didn't remember anything after he'd come the night before. He had been exhausted by the long day. That thought woke him up completely as he recalled why the day had seemed so long. Rolling over, he shut off the alarm then stared down at Saul's still-sleeping form.

Saul had not been kidding about not being a morning person. The alarm usually went off for a while before Saul even twitched. When they were together, he usually turned it off and went to make breakfast for the two of them. Today, he took a few extra moments to enjoy the view. His. Saul Valencia was his to look at and touch and love. He had been the dream—a dream Lee hadn't thought he would or could ever have.

Amazingly, Saul had turned out to be an even better human being in real life than he was in Lee's fantasies. When did that ever happen? He had been so afraid that

Saul was going to be a complete asshole. *How did I get so lucky?*

Saul stirred and peeked up at Lee through slitted eyes. "Why are you staring?" Saul rasped in his husky morning voice.

"I'm counting my blessings. My mom always used to say to count your blessings, not your problems. She said she heard it somewhere and it always stuck with her." Lee paused so he could get the rest of it out. "Even when she was dying, she still said it, said that she had lived a good life and had had many blessings." Lee shrugged. "I didn't get it at the time. How can you be thankful for blessings when you're dying? But I get what she was trying to say now, even though I can't say I'm all that religious."

Lee paused again to gather his thoughts as a definitely more awake Saul raised his hand to rest it on Lee's cheek. He took a deep breath and raised his own hand to place it over Saul's before he continued. "There are problems, big problems ahead of us, but what I'm thinking about right now is how thankful I am for the blessing of you."

Lee was horrified to see a tear trickle from Saul's eye. "Why are you crying? I didn't mean to make you sad."

"This isn't a sad tear. It's a happy one, a term I never understood before now. Why would you cry if you were happy?" Saul raised his other hand to dash at his tears, before using the hand cupping the side of Lee's face to pull him down into a soft kiss before looking into his eyes. "I will do my best to always be a blessing to you. I love you."

"I love you too."

The moment was broken by Saul's second alarm going off, making both of them jump.

"I'll go start breakfast, if you want to jump in the shower first," Lee offered.

"Sounds like a plan." Saul pulled Lee in for a hug before releasing him and allowing Lee to get up.

After putting on a pair of boxers and a quick stop in the bathroom to empty his bladder and brush his teeth, Lee made his way to the kitchen, just as Saul started to shave with his electric razor. His first task was to get the coffee started. Sappy conversation first thing in the morning or not, Saul was a definite addict and Lee was sure Saul would be looking for the hot brew as soon as he finished his shower. Looking in the refrigerator, he brought out bacon and eggs and had the bacon mostly done by the time Saul came out.

Lee hid a smile as Saul made a beeline for the coffee pot and poured a cup, sipping it black before he spoke to Lee.

"Here. I'll take over. You go jump in the shower."

"You sure you're caffeinated enough to finish the bacon and cook the eggs?"

"I'll muddle through somehow, smartass. Get your butt in gear."

Lee chuckled all the way to the shower, hurrying through his morning routine when he saw the time. After getting dressed, he rushed out to the kitchen. "We have to leave in, like, ten minutes if we're going to have time to swing through a coffee place and get coffee for Gracie."

"That's the great thing about the airport here. There's a Starbucks right at the arrivals gate. We just need to drive there, park and go in to wait for her."

"Really? I didn't know that."

"When was the last time you flew?" Saul asked as he placed the filled plates on the breakfast bar and poured more coffee in his mug before joining Lee at the bar where filled glasses of orange juice already sat.

"I've never been on a plane. My family always drove for vacations and we haven't gone anywhere since Mom died."

"Do you have a passport?"

"Nope."

"We need to fix that."

"I'm game. There are definitely a ton of places I would love to see, but I didn't really want to go alone."

"I'll be happy to be your travel companion, dear sir," Saul said. "What is number one on your travel list? Hold that thought. Focus on eating. I just realized the time. We can talk on the ride to the airport."

With a nod, Lee dug into the food on his plate, so they could get going.

Once in the car, Saul picked the conversation back up. "Where would you go if you could go anywhere?"

"I've always dreamed of going to Ireland. It's where my mom's family was from. That's the side of the family where I get the lovely red hair and fair skin that burns in March." Lee gave a self-deprecating laugh at the admission.

"Yeah, I still can't believe you blistered that day we went to the amusement park in late September."

"I know, right? But I should have known better. Anyway, I've always wanted to go to see Ireland. Oh, and Paris is also on my list. What about you?"

"I've never been to Ireland or Paris. I would be interested in going to both. I'd also like to take you to some of my favorite places in Italy. My parents took us a couple of times to see family. I think you would really love Florence and Milan. Florence has this artistic feel I think you'd enjoy. Milan is just Milan. There's no place in the world like it."

"Sounds good to me." Lee paused before asking, "Is there anything we need to discuss before we pick up Gracie?"

"Not that I can think of at the moment. Relax and enjoy the ride and conversation, babe. I'm sure we'll do nothing but talk about the situation for hours. I have no idea what everyone is going to suggest. We'll have to wait and see. Just be you and I'm sure Gracie is going to love you. Okay?"

"Yeah, okay." Lee still fretted the rest of the ride to the airport, but he tried to hide it as best he could. Luckily it wasn't a very long trip to get there. After parking on the parking deck, they made their way to the arrivals area where people were standing around waiting, some with signs, some without. Everyone's eyes were trained on the hallway coming from the gates, though.

"What kind of coffee does Gracie want? I can go get it, since I have no idea what she looks like and she should be coming any minute."

Saul handed Lee his phone with a text message saying exactly what she wanted. It was a good thing too. *What. The. Hell?* The order was a 'venti vanilla bean cappuccino skinny with two extra shots of espresso'.

"I'm taking your phone with me. This is crazy."

Saul laughed at him. "Only for you weirdos who don't drink coffee."

"Yeah well, I don't have to speak in tongues to ask for a Coke, now, do I?"

Saul just laughed harder. "Could you get me a venti americano while you're there, please?"

Lee rolled his eyes at his insane boyfriend before turning and making his way to the line. He managed to get the orders placed and retrieved and was almost back to Saul when Saul was suddenly tackle-hugged by a woman who he assumed was Gracie, since Saul was hugging her back. From the way everyone talked about her, he'd expected Gracie to be a six-foot-tall Amazonian. What he got instead was a woman who only came up to Saul's chest, even while wearing what appeared to be four-inch heels.

"Saul, I'm so happy to see you again. Where's my coffee?"

Saul indicated Lee behind her. Gracie spun around and snagged a cup from Lee's hand, taking a big sip. "That is *not* a venti vanilla bean cappuccino skinny with two extra shots of espresso. What are you trying to do to me?"

Lee quickly looked at the cup he still had in his hand. "You took Saul's coffee. This one's yours." Lee handed her the remaining cup as Gracie thrust the one in her hand at Saul. "How can you drink that? It's like drinking coffee-flavored water."

"It is not," Saul said with a laugh.

"Close enough," Gracie said as she sipped her coffee. "Ahhh. That's much better."

"Didn't you have any coffee before you got on the plane?"

"Of course I did. This is, like, my sixth cup today."

"I think you might have a problem, Gracie."

Lee chuckled. "Like you can talk."

Saul shot Lee a grin. "My blood is only, like, thirty percent coffee. I think Gracie's blood is eighty-five or ninety percent coffee."

Lee looked at Gracie to see how she took that pronouncement. "What? I can't dispute it. He's probably right." Gracie then cackled loudly, the sound echoing through the terminal. She didn't seem to care a bit that everyone turned to stare at her. "Gracie Stalone... Nice to meet you. You must be Lee." Gracie then thrust her hand at Lee to shake.

"Yes, ma'am. I've heard a lot about you. It's very nice to meet you."

"Ma'am? You have a polite one here, Sauly, and he is very, very pretty. It looks like you've done well this time. I approve, but time's a-wasting, boys. Let's get this show on the road."

Gracie handed Saul her carryon and Lee her laptop case before turning and heading toward the doors leading outside to the parking garage. Lee and Saul had to run to catch up. *Man, she can move quick.*

The retrieval of the car and the trip back to the office were fast, with Gracie entertaining the two of them with her latest stories of weird requests from her clients.

"Did he really expect the team to pay for his wife to fly to all of his games?"

"Yep. My client firmly believes she is his good luck charm. I tried to talk him out of it. He insisted. The team, of course, said no, but I soothed the sting by negotiating a million-dollar sign-on bonus instead."

Lee laughed. "I'm sure that helped."

Gracie turned from where she was sitting in the front passenger seat to waggle her eyebrows at Lee as they pulled into the garage at the back of the building. Lee hopped out and opened the door for Gracie, then offered her a hand out of the car.

"My, my, what a gentleman. You sure you're gay, honey? I'm currently on the market for husband number five."

"I'm sure I'm gay. Sorry."

"Hands off, Gracie. This one's mine."

"Story of my life. All the good ones are either taken or gay."

"In this case, it's both," Saul quipped.

"Yeah. Yeah. Rub it in. We have twenty minutes before the lawyer gets here. I've simply been dying to see the mural Lee painted for your store."

Lee said, "It's next door. Saul can take you. I'll take your stuff to the conference room then head to the breakroom to start some coffee."

"You're speaking my language. Saul, let's go."

Lee snagged the bags and made his way through the side entrance into the office building, dropping the bags off in the conference room. Hearing voices, he followed the sound to the break area, where Eric was already busy making coffee and Kirk was sitting at one of the breakroom tables.

"Oh, good. I was going to start some coffee, but you beat me to it. Saul took Gracie next door to see the mural. What are you doing here, Kirk? I thought you were going into the shop."

"The guys can handle it. Eric and I talked, and we figured it would be better if I was part of the discussions and to be here, so you have someone to support you too. This group can be a little pushy. Eric's mom is watching the girls for us."

"Thank you. That means a lot, Kirk. I appreciate it more than you know." Lee turned toward Eric and changed the subject before he could embarrass himself. "I have a feeling we're going to go through a lot of coffee today. I hope you have enough in stock. Gracie alone can probably drink that one pot you just made Eric."

"Yeah. We always joke that we're going to save some time and set her up with an IV filled with coffee."

"I could see that. Man, she's scary as hell and yet I adore her already."

"I told you." Eric looked over his shoulder at Lee and gave him a smirk. "She's one of the most amazingly organized people I have ever met and will bend over backward to help you if you are one of her people, but she *is* scary."

"Talking about me again, Eric?" Gracie asked as she breezed through the doorway. How they hadn't heard her coming in those heels, Lee didn't know.

"You know it," Eric said, walking over to give Gracie a hug, picking her right off the ground and spinning her in a circle.

Once he'd set her down, Gracie grabbed his cheeks and pulled him down to smack him on the lips. "You ready to run off with me and be husband number five? That one already turned me down." Gracie waved a hand in Lee's general direction as she spoke.

"Sadly, Gracie love, I'm afraid you've missed your chance. I'm an engaged man."

"Woot! Kirk's making an honest man of you?"

"I am," Kirk said, leaning down to kiss Gracie's cheek. "Nice to see you again, Gracie."

"Nice to see you too, love. When's the happy event? I'd better get an invite."

"We're still trying to decide, and of course you're getting an invitation," Eric answered. "Top of the list. The girls were very excited to hear you were in town this weekend."

"And how are my Claire-bear and Sammy-Sam?"

"They're doing well. Had some drama a couple of weeks ago, but we're working through it. I'm adopting Sam after the wedding and Kirk's going to adopt Claire. We will be a family of four. I hope you have time for dinner at our place during this visit."

"I'm yours for at least the weekend. I have a reservation at some fancy hotel spa place near here."

"Great! Then how about everyone planning on coming over for a barbecue tonight? Saul, why don't you call your parents and invite your sister and her family too."

"They'll actually be here shortly, so you can invite them yourself." They were interrupted by the sound of a door buzzer. "That's either them or Jeff. Let me go let in whoever it is."

Lee rolled his lips between his teeth to stop from laughing when he looked over at Eric.

"What?"

"That shade of lipstick, while gorgeous on Gracie, is soooo not your color."

Eric looked at his reflection in the shiny surface of the paper towel dispenser and chuckled at the view before reaching for a paper towel, wetting it at the sink and using it to wipe off his mouth. When he was done, he threw the used paper towel in the trash and grabbed the completed coffee, pouring it into the waiting carafe and starting another pot.

"Hey, Lee, can you grab the creamers and sugar and stuff? I'll go ahead and take the coffee into the conference room."

"Can you point me in the direction of the little agent's room on the way?"

"I'll show you, Gracie," Kirk said, following his fiancé through the door.

Lee grabbed the requested items then set them on the counter. Then he placed both hands on the countertop and hung his head for a moment. He'd been surrounded by people until this moment and it all suddenly hit him. *This is big!* Saul wanted him to be at his side as he came out. There was a lawyer and an agent involved and Saul's family and Eric and Kirk and the guys at the garage.

Saul circled Lee from behind with strong arms, halting his racing thoughts. "You okay, babe?"

"I just don't want to let everyone down. You're doing this for me, to protect me from my psychotic brother."

"That's one way to look at it."

"How else can you look at it?" Lee turned around in Saul's embrace so he could see his lover's expression.

"You could also look at it as you are being my supportive partner, enabling me to be strong enough to come out publicly."

"But you're only doing it because of Frank. I'm endangering everyone. You and Eric could lose business. Kirk could lose business, all because of me."

"Wow. Drama queen much?" Gracie's voice startled him from the doorway. She came over and pushed her way between the two men, facing Lee. "And how much would it have meant to you to have a gay role model growing up? A big strong, manly man to show you that gay comes in all shapes and sizes."

"It would have meant a lot." Lee couldn't deny that.

"Even though he never specifically told me he was gay until last night, I knew, and I have watched Saul struggle with the decision to come out or not come out since college. It's not like he's doing this on a whim. I wouldn't support him if that was what was happening. It's time, especially if your brother is trying to use Saul's fame to hurt you. Saul is too much of a protector to allow any of his loved ones to be hurt on his watch. It's one of the things I most admire about him. It's what made him a great linebacker, his sense of pride and sense of responsibility for that or whomever he has deemed important."

"But the others…"

"The others are all adults and have decided to stand in solidarity with Saul." Gracie paused, making sure she had Lee's attention. "And you. You are part of this family that Saul and Eric have created by choice and that's not even including Saul's monstrous family by blood. You have to remember that you're not alone anymore.

"Can you give us a few minutes, Gracie?"

"You get five then we'll expect you in the conference room."

Lee watched Gracie as she walked out of the door.

"What brought this on? I thought we were on the same page."

"We are. I panicked, thinking about everything going on. I don't bring much to the table." Lee shrugged at the end, not really sure what he was trying to say. Everything was jumbled in his head.

"You bring *you*. You're so amazing to me. Your drawing talent is awe-inspiring. Gracie was beyond impressed. She wants to represent you."

Lee laughed at that. "Yeah, right."

"It's true. You can ask her."

"But you've seen and done so much, played a professional sport and earned a lot of money and traveled to all those places you were telling me about on the ride to the airport. You've started a business. I mean, I never really thought about the age difference between us until yesterday. I felt so young, crying all over your mama. I felt so amazing when you told me you loved me, and I do believe what I said this morning. I just don't want anyone to look at me and wonder what the hell you're doing with me. I'm a mechanic. My hands are dirty most of the time and I shop at Walmart for most of my clothes."

"It doesn't make sense for you to spend a ton of money on your clothes. You're an artist and a mechanic, both messy career choices, but you're doing the two things you love the most. Do you know how many people search their whole lives, trying to find what or who makes them happy? While I'm good at breaking things, I suck at fixing things. Hell, I don't even know how to change a tire, that's why I have AAA."

"Well, we'll have to fix that. You should at least know how to change a tire."

"Me and my big mouth." Saul smirked at Lee as he said it, though, so he must not be too upset. "Anyway, if it truly bothers you, we can get you new clothes for when we go out if it would make you more comfortable. They don't really have a lot of clothes to fit me at Walmart or I would— Check that. I probably still wouldn't shop there. But clothes don't make the man. I adore you as you are, because you fit me better than any clothes. We can talk about anything and you are willing to try everything. I can't wait to show you the favorite places I've been and discover new ones together."

"I can't wait either."

"As far as being young, you are. There's no getting around that. You'll grow and change, as will I. We both have a lifetime of growing and firsts ahead of us and I would like to plan to do them together, if you don't mind."

"I don't mind at all." Lee leaned in and hugged Saul while breathing in his scent.

Saul spoke into Lee's hair. "Talk to me. Don't shut me out. Okay?"

"Okay." Lee relaxed further into Saul's embrace.

"Break it up, you two." Lee and Saul both turned at the sound of Eric's voice. "Gracie has sent me to tell you your five minutes are up. Your family is all here. Mama brought food, so we're ready to get started."

Chapter Twelve

The meeting was loud, as Saul had expected. There were too many opinionated individuals in one space for it to be any other way.

Saul offered, "We could have me do a proposal and post it online — a lot of people are coming out that way — then release a statement."

Lee's shouted "No" silenced the room. He flushed purple, glancing wildly from face to face before standing up and fleeing out of the door.

Saul stood up to follow, but Kirk held out a hand to stop him. "Let me talk to him, see what's going on in his head."

Saul stood stock still, torn by indecision. Every instinct said he should follow Kirk and be the one to talk to Lee. His mama's arm slipping around his waist made him tear his gaze from the door to look at her.

"I love you, son."

"I love you t—"

Saul was interrupted by his mama. "But you are a dumbass."

"What?"

"I have only known Lee for a short time, but even I know he would not want such a private moment made public. He has an artist's soul."

"Oh." Saul hadn't thought of it that way.

"I know you've decided he's yours and that man loves you something fierce, but you are not doing a great job with the wooing, son. Maybe you should talk to your father and see about getting some tips. He still woos me. Why, just last week—"

Saul held up his hand. "I've got it. I screwed up, but we have talked about it before."

"But have you *romanced* him?"

Saul's cheeks heated in embarrassment. "No. I've basically just told him I want to marry him." Mama raised an imperious eyebrow at him, and Saul looked away from her stare only to be met by the angry faces of the other people in the room. "I know. I know. I hear you. I'll fix it."

Lee and Kirk came back in. "Sorry, everyone," Lee said quietly, his head hanging.

"No, babe." Saul strode over to Lee and yanked him into his arms. "I'm the one who is sorry. You're right. When I ask—and make no mistake, I will be asking." Saul grabbed Lee's chin and made him look at him, pausing to give Lee a gentle kiss before he said, "It will not and should not be as a part of all this. When I ask, it'll be a moment of pure joy, without any of this other drama hanging over our heads. Okay?"

"Yeah." Lee nodded before giving Saul a huge hug, burying his face in the crook of his neck. Saul just took a moment to savor the feel of having Lee in his arms.

Gracie clapped her hands together, interrupting the moment. "Alrighty then. Let's figure out something that works for everyone. A proposal is off the table. What about an Instagram post of the two of you? You said you were moving in together earlier. How about something about that? Then maybe schedule an interview. I have some great contacts. I could make a few phone calls and see if any of them would be interested."

"Sergei is also my client," Jeff spoke up. "I can contact him and let him know about Lee not working for his father anymore. It's really Frank's mess to sort out about the deposit. He won't have anything on Lee after Saul comes out."

"Well, what is everyone standing around for?" Mama said after a moment of silence. "Chop-chop. Let's make this happen, people. Lee and Saul, go upstairs and decide where you want the picture taken. Lexie, go with them so you can take the picture. Gracie, make that call. Jeff, you make your call. The rest of us will make a list for the barbecue tonight so we can go shopping."

"We have a surprise for you after this is over, Mama and Papa," Saul said.

"For us? What kind of surprise? You know I don't like surprises."

"You'd better move before the lightning gets ya, Mama." Lexie chuckled from her spot next to Saul and Lee at the door.

"What?" Mama asked, all innocence. "It's true."

"You don't dislike surprises, my love. It's the not knowing that kills you." Papa cackled, which earned him a smack to the chest from his wife.

"Oh, stop, you."

Papa pulled Mama to his side and kissed the side of her head. "But I wouldn't change a thing about you, my love."

"On that note, let's get our part done." Saul grabbed Lee's hand and pulled him out of the door and toward the back of the building, where the door leading upstairs was located. Lee tugged on his hand to stop him before he could put in the code for the reader.

"What's up?"

"I'm sorry, but I really don't want people to see any part of our home. If you still want me to move in, that is, after my freak-out?"

It killed Saul to see the uncertainty come back. "Of course I still want you to move in with me and you're right. Private is private." Saul paused to think a moment. "What do you think about taking the picture in front of the mural at the store?"

Lexie added, "That will give us a reason to post the picture, saying how proud of your boyfriend you are too for doing such a fantastic job."

"Would that be okay?" Saul asked. "Because I am so very proud of you. It wouldn't be a lie and it wouldn't be in our home. Everyone can see the mural. It's public."

Saul held his breath as he waited for Lee's response. After a moment, Lee nodded, finally looking up and shyly making eye contact. "That would be good. Maybe it will get people in to see it and offset some of the bad press."

"There ya go. That's a good way to look at it." Lexie cheered.

"Great. Let's head over to the store then and get the picture done. Maybe one of the whole mural and one of the two of us together."

"Yeah, let's go."

Saul and Lee had fun taking the pictures with Lexie, posing in different positions and with different expressions on their faces. Lexie acted the role of famous photographer, hamming it up for the patrons of the store.

After the pictures were taken, they returned to the group to find everyone buzzing with excitement. "What's going on?"

Gracie was doing a little jig as she replied, "Your agent is amazing. That's what."

"And modest too," Saul said with a chuckle.

"If you got it, flaunt it. You two will be singing my praises in a moment. I, your fantabulous agent, have gotten you a sit-down interview with Vera Iverson."

"The host of the talk show *Hear Me Speak*?"

"That's the one, kiddo."

"Why would she want to have me on her show?"

"Well, timing is everything. She is doing a week of shows about being gay in professional sports. She is beyond excited to include you and do your exclusive first interview."

"When?"

"You need to fly out to New York city on Tuesday night. The show is being recorded Wednesday morning for broadcast Wednesday afternoon. She has other gay professional athletes on her show Monday and Tuesday, both male and female."

"Wow, that's fast," Lee said, looking a little more overwhelmed than Saul would have liked. "And do they still want us to post the Instagram photo?"

"They do. Then they can promote the exclusive interview this week, during Monday's and Tuesday's shows."

"Oh, okay."

Lexie waved Saul's phone at Gracie. "I got a lot of great shots. Which ones do you think we should post?"

Gracie took the phone, with Mama looking over her shoulder. "Wait. I thought you were going to take the pictures upstairs in your apartment?"

"Lee and I decided we didn't want strangers to see our home. Friends and family only are allowed. We decided to take the pictures in front of the mural instead. I'm very proud of him and the work he did on it. It's a legitimate reason to post."

Gracie stared for a moment before grinning. "That's brilliant. Wish I'd thought of that."

"It was actually Lee's inspired work that gave us the idea."

"Well done, Lee. Maybe we'll get you some commissions out of this too."

"Oh, I didn't mean…"

Gracie went over to take Lee's hands in hers. "You are an extremely talented artist. I saw what you did here and Eric showed me pictures of the mural in the girls' playroom, as well as the paintwork you did on the motorcycle at Kirk's shop. I'm beyond impressed and, believe me, I'm not easy to impress."

"Told you she loved the mural and wanted to represent you." Saul couldn't help but be charmed by the shy pleasure on Lee's face at being complimented.

"But I don't even have training. I only took a few classes at the community college. I just do it for fun. I'm a mechanic."

"And an artist," everyone said at once, making Lee jump.

"Can we *not* talk about it right now?" Lee said, waving his hands around. "Let's just handle one life-changing event at a time, please." Lee gave Saul a pleading look that Saul couldn't resist.

"Subject changed for now. Jeff, while they're deciding on the pictures, did you get a hold of Sergei?"

"Yes, and let's just say he wasn't too happy with the news that Lee didn't even work for Clark and Sons. It seems Frank has been giving him quite the run-around and it isn't just one motorcycle, it's two. He was going to send some of his men over to collect his bikes and bring them over to Kirk's. He wants to meet with Lee on Monday morning, if that's okay?"

"Kirk? Am I free Monday?"

Kirk gave him an 'are you freaking kidding me?' look. "We'll make time for him. Sergei is one of the richest men in the city. If we can get his business, it's a very good thing."

"Yes," Jeff said, adjusting his glasses. "I hope you don't mind, but I took the liberty of explaining to Sergei exactly why you no longer work with your father and brother. His exact reaction was, 'So what?' As long as you do good work, he has no problem giving you his business. He hasn't been happy with the quality of work at Clark and Sons of late."

"Yeah, I always used to do all the service on Sergei's vehicles. He has quite a few."

"That's what he figured when I told him how long you've been working at Everyone's Mechanic. As for you, Saul, Sergei says he wished he had known your" — Jeff cleared his throat with a cough — "leanings, before you were taken. He always very much enjoyed watching you play."

Saul stared at his lawyer in shock, absolutely speechless. "Um, thank you for squaring everything with Sergei for us. That's great news about the work for

Kirk's shop. I have no idea how to even respond to the other," Saul said. "So again, subject change." He turned to Gracie and his mama. "What picture or pictures and what caption? Have we decided?"

"Yep. We think these two here." Gracie held the phone out so Lee and Saul could see. "The one of the mural at the store and this other one where you have your arms around each other, standing next to it. The first picture should be the mural, saying something like *'Look what my talented boyfriend did for our flagship store. Come see it at…'* and give the address of the store. Then post the second picture of you and Lee, with you saying something like *'So proud to be dating this amazingly talented human being.'* Any objections? Other thoughts?"

"I don't have any. Lee?"

"Nope. Let's just do this and get it over with. I'm tired of thinking about it."

"Okay. Hand me my phone and I'll upload them to Instagram and Twitter. In for a penny and all that." Saul typed into his phone. "And done." He then took a deep breath, staring at his Instagram post as it finished loading. "I just came out." A big ball of emotion came out of nowhere. "Holy shit, I just came out. I don't know why I'm crying." Saul dashed at the tears on his face. Suddenly Lee was there, pushing into his arms.

"Sh-h, babe. It's okay."

Saul lost the battle with his tears and lowered his head to Lee's shoulder, letting all the emotion work through him. His sobs racked his body. The only thing keeping him grounded in that moment was the feel of Lee's arms around him and the murmur of his lover's voice. Finally, the storm was spent and he lifted his head to find the room empty, except for the two of them.

Lee leaned over to the conference table and snagged a couple of napkins from the pile, before handing them to Saul so he could blow his nose and wipe his eyes.

"Sorry, Lee. I didn't mean to lose it like that."

"You have nothing to be sorry for. In fact, I should be the one apologizing to you."

"What? Why?" Saul was honestly perplexed by that one. What on earth did Lee have to be sorry about?

"I've been so busy fighting my own demons that I didn't even really think about the fact that this was a big deal for you too. At the same time, it makes me feel a little better to know I'm not the only one nervous about all this. You were so matter-of-fact about it all. Does that make me a horrible boyfriend?"

Saul gave a watery chuckle. "Not at all. I understand completely. I was trying to be strong, but this is big."

"It is — and kind of hard to take back. I mean, if we hurry, we might be able to delete the posts, if you want. Do you want?"

Saul evaluated his feelings. "No. We'll ride it out. It was time. I think part of my meltdown was from the feeling of relief that I no longer have to hide. Does that make sense?"

"It does. I'm proud of you."

"You are?"

"Yep. That took a lot of guts. You have a ton of followers. I don't even have an Instagram account. In case I haven't said it, I'm very proud and happy to be your boyfriend."

"That's very good to hear. It's going to be a little rough for the next little bit."

"I know and I'll be here with you every step of the way."

"Does that mean you're flying up to New York with me Tuesday night?"

"Do you want me to?"

"I would like nothing more. Maybe we can go up Monday night and I can show you some of the sights."

"You don't think that will be a problem?"

"Nah. It's New York. New Yorkers don't care."

"All clear in here?" Eric's voice questioned through the doorway.

"Yeah. We're good," Lee called back, stepping away from Saul.

"I was just poking my head in to tell you that everyone is heading over to show your parents the surprise. Mama is dying to know. We thought the two of you might need some downtime before the barbecue."

"That sounds good, actually," Saul said with a yawn. "All of a sudden I'm exhausted for some reason."

"Gee, I wonder why?" Eric's voice dripped with sarcasm as he asked the question before stepping up and pulling Saul into a hug. "Proud of you, buddy. I know this wasn't easy, but it's done now." Saul sagged in Eric's arms.

"Yeah. Now let's see what happens next."

"Hand me your phone and head upstairs. Gracie said she'll monitor the response for you. We'll call Lee's phone if we need you."

"Sounds good."

"Great. See you at the house at six. That should give you guys time to rest. We'll give you a status report when you get there. Here, Lee. Let me help you get him upstairs. I think he's done."

Saul focused on putting one foot in front of the other, through the door leading to his apartment, up the stairs and to his bedroom. Hands were on him, stripping his clothes off down to his underwear then he was on the bed with the covers being tucked around him. "Don't leave, Lee," he managed to mumble and stay awake long enough to hear Lee's response.

"I'm not. I'm just going to see Eric out and grab us some water bottles. I'll be right back."

"Okay." Saul thought he said it out loud, but maybe not, as he faded to sleep.

Chapter Thirteen

Lee stared through the window of the airplane at the view of the city. The cars looked like little ants rushing around, even at ten o'clock at night.

"What do you think, babe?" Saul whispered in his ear, leaning in to look out of the window with him.

"It's amazing." Lee tried to crane his neck to see as much as he possibly could.

Saul chuckled in his ear, making Lee shiver. "Wait until we actually land, and you're in the middle of it all."

Lee sat back in his chair, checking his seatbelt before turning to look at Saul. "Thanks for bringing me with you."

"I wouldn't have it any other way. I need you with me on this."

"At least the feedback has been mostly positive."

"There is that. I've been pleasantly surprised by the support."

"Well, except that one guy." Lee grimaced. "Sorry I mentioned it."

"It's all good. I never would've guessed John was such a homophobic ass, though. I mean, we roomed together on road trips for the entire time I was in the league. We were never best buds or anything, but we coexisted pretty well."

"Sorry, but you did get some really great responses from some of the others."

"Yeah. I was really happy to hear from Coach. I didn't even realize he had a gay son. It was awesome to hear it led to a great discussion between them."

"See? You're already making a difference."

"I hope so. I'm lucky to have such a great family, a fantastic circle of friends and especially you to support me through this. I can't even imagine if I didn't have all of you." Saul reached out, took Lee's hand and squeezed. Lee squeezed back.

"Speaking of family, I'm so glad Lexie recorded your parents' response to the surprise."

Saul chuckled. "Yeah, that was pretty epic. I've never seen Mama speechless before. She was so happy."

"Your dad was pretty stoked too. That kind of surprised me."

"Dad really likes it here. He loves the fact that there are seasons. Florida is nice, but it's pretty humid and unbearable during the summer. Now that they're retired, there's no reason they couldn't spend the summers in North Carolina, get a break from the humidity and away from all the tourists."

"Yep. Your mama seemed most excited about being able to go shopping for furniture."

"My mama just likes to shop. Period. Now she has a valid reason."

Lee couldn't help but smile to see Saul so amused. He'd been really concerned when Saul seemed to almost collapse into bed Saturday afternoon after the postings online. He'd had to wake Saul in time for them to get ready for the barbecue. He'd made a promise to himself to keep a better eye on Saul in the future. He was obviously much too good at hiding his worries.

"Hey, why the scowl?" Saul ran his finger between Lee's eyebrows as he asked, making Lee realize that he was indeed scowling.

"Thinking about how well you hid your worries from me and how we both need to work on talking to each other more."

"Seems to be a pretty constant theme, doesn't it? But if it's any consolation, I hid them from myself too. Buried them deep, something I tend to do. I spend a lot of time worrying. I take care of others and I forget to take care of myself." Saul shrugged. "I'll work on it."

"And, as your boyfriend, I'll help you. We're partners. You can talk to me and I can share the load."

"You do, and I couldn't do this without you."

"You mean you wouldn't have to do this without me." Lee gave a self-deprecating laugh.

"If it wasn't your brother, it would have been someone else threatening to expose my secret, Lee." Saul made air quotes around the word 'secret'. "Not that it was much of one. My friends and family already knew."

"True." Lee chuckled. "I can't believe your nephews and Claire and Sam made that huge sign for the barbecue that said *Happy Coming Out Day*. That was epic."

"I know, right? I didn't even know they sold that much glitter." Saul started to laugh, which set Lee off until they were both laughing hard. By the time they had themselves under control, it was time to get off the plane.

Lee was further amazed and frankly a little terrified when they were in their taxi heading to their hotel. "Do all taxi drivers drive like race car drivers?"

"That has been my experience, yes. Don't worry. He's a professional. He'll get us there in one piece."

"Good to know." Lee had to admit, if only to himself, that he'd been worried about it.

Saul took his hand and raised it to his lips. "Thanks for coming with me."

"Nowhere else I'd rather be."

Arriving at the hotel, they went to the check-in desk.

"Welcome to New York, Mr. Valencia. We have your reservation all set for two nights. If I could just see an ID and get a credit card for incidentals."

Saul handed over his card and ID and, within minutes, they were on their way up in the elevator to the top floor. Lee was astounded to see the size of the room, when they entered.

"Wow, this is amazing. I don't think I've ever seen something so fancy." Lee was a little afraid to touch anything, actually. He wandered from the main area to the opulent bathroom, which had all sorts of shiny surfaces, then back into the main area.

Saul came in and pulled him into his arms. "Gracie made the reservations. She must have decided we needed a touch of fancy for this trip." Saul shrugged. "Let's just enjoy it. Now, I don't know about you, but I'm starving. How about we order some room service — or better yet, how about I order room service for the both of us. Room service prices tend to be a little high and I don't want you freaking out."

"Okay. Let's go with option number two. You order. You know what I like."

"Yep and I'm so lucky one of those things is me." Saul gave him a boyish grin and a peck on the lips before going to look for the menu. Saul placed the order while Lee hung up their clothes from their carryon bags. Lee had been whisked away on a speedy shopping spree by Saul's mama on Sunday for outfits for the trip. He'd been thankful she hadn't gone too fancy, although he had a feeling the clothes weren't cheap, especially as she hadn't let him see the price tags.

Once the food arrived, they sat down at the little table to eat. Saul had gotten them steak, baked potatoes and a salad to share. Lee hadn't realized how hungry he was until the smell hit him, then he was starving. He had to consciously slow down when he realized he was eating way too fast. Saul was obviously starving too, since neither of them spoke for the first five minutes of devouring their meals.

"By the way, we never talked about it, but whatever happened with Sergei this morning?"

Lee had to chuckle as he remembered it. "Sergei came in with, like, four other guys, two of them rolling in his motorcycles. One of these motorcycles is worth more than some houses around Raleigh." Lee had to shake his head at that. "Anyway, we went to Kirk's office and we talked about what he wanted done on each. It's going to be an amazing project to work on. I did some rough sketches, based on what he'd described. He loved them and gave me the go-ahead. He wasn't nearly as scary as I expected him to be from the way everyone talked about him. His accent was amazing. I don't know why I didn't expect him to have one."

"You never met him before? I thought you did all of his auto work?"

"I did, but Frank took all the credit for it. I mainly kept my head down and did my job. It was easier that way," Lee answered with a grimace. "Oh, I did find out he gave Frank a five-thousand-dollar deposit. Sergei said for me not to worry about that part, that it's between him and Frank." Lee shrugged. "It's hard not to worry, though."

"But Frank made that mess."

"I know, but he's still family, and I've been taking care of him and my dad since Mom died—before, actually. I was the one who did all the groceries and the laundry. I did the books at the shop too. Dad was hopeless at it and Frank didn't care. Frank worked harder at trying not to do work than he did at working."

"Why am I not surprised at that from the little you've told me about him?" Saul shook his head in disappointment. "But remember… They threw you out, Lee. They are no longer your responsibility. Keeping an eye on me is a full-time job. If it would make you feel better to take over doing the laundry, I won't fight you on it. I hate it."

"Really? I enjoy it. You start with a pile and you sort it and wash it and fold it and put it away. There's a rhythm to it. I hate grocery shopping."

"Huh. I enjoy grocery shopping, especially at some of the specialty stores where you get to sample new stuff."

"I'll do laundry and you can do the shopping, then."

"Sounds like a plan to me."

Lee couldn't help but chuckle. "What?"

"Here we are in a luxurious hotel, eating room service in front of a window with a fantastic view of the city, and we're discussing laundry."

Saul smirked at him. "True, but that's life, isn't it? It's kind of like a house. The exciting moments — trips to new places and meeting people and trying new things — are like the finishes or the top floors with a view, but you couldn't have all that without the foundation. The foundation is created by your friends and family and work and all the little things like laundry and shopping and cleaning the house. Not exciting, but necessary. They're what really give your life meaning. The rest is just decoration."

"Listen to you, Mr. Philosophical," Lee teased. "I like it, though, and I'm happy to be part of your foundation."

"You are a new, but very important part. I am excited to spend this time building our foundation, but I promise that after we finish dinner, we'll spend some time enjoying this wonderful view too."

Lee nodded. "I can get behind that plan."

* * * *

Lee stood on the observation deck of the Empire State Building trying to relax a moment. When Saul had said he would play tour guide, Lee hadn't known he meant try to show him the whole city in one day — or at least it felt like it.

They had been up at seven to get to the ferry to head out to Ellis Island to see the Statue of Liberty up close and personal. It had been quite amazing, seeing something he had only ever seen on TV or in movies. And they had perfect weather for it, not too hot and not freezing. A car and driver had been waiting for them when they got back to take them on a tour of different neighborhoods and sights. Now they were on top of the Empire State Building and the view was spectacular.

"What do you want to do next?" Saul asked from beside him. "I can see about getting us tickets to a Broadway show tonight, if you want?"

"I really just want to go back to the hotel and take a nap."

Saul laughed. "Yeah. It has been a lot, hasn't it?"

"It really has. We can come back, can't we? Do things like a show and all that then? I think I'm just done, and we have a big day tomorrow."

"Yeah. You're right. I guess I've gotten a little carried away."

Lee held up his hand, showing an inch of space between his finger and thumb before splaying his finger and thumb wider apart. Achieving his goal of making Saul laugh, he reached out to take Saul's hand in his. "Come on. Let's go back to the hotel."

When they exited the elevator, they were greeted by a crowd of paparazzi. Camera flashes were going off and questions were being shouted at them. Lee froze in a combination of equal parts terror and shock. He'd been tense at the beginning of the day expecting something like this to happen around every corner, but when nothing had happened, he'd relaxed his guard, thinking that Saul really did know what he was talking about and New Yorkers just didn't care.

Lee let himself be led toward the exit, Saul's bulk making a great shield as they pushed through the crowd of paparazzi. It also allowed Lee to hide behind him. Security guards arrived and escorted Saul and Lee to their waiting car and driver. Lee took great gulping breaths of air once the car had pulled away from the curb, leaving the crowd behind.

"You did great, babe."

"That was scary as hell," Lee finally got out. "I thought New Yorkers didn't care."

"They usually don't," Saul answered with a shrug. "I'll call Gracie and find out what's going on once we get back to our room."

Lee paced the hotel room when they made it back, thankfully without further run-ins. Saul was on the phone with Gracie and Lee wasn't able to glean much from the 'uh-huhs' and 'reallys' coming from Saul's end of the conversation.

"Hey, Lee, do you know whose number is 919-555-5555?"

"That's Frank's number. Why?"

"It's Frank's number, Gracie." Pause. "I'll ask him. Did you ever used to be on the same phone plan as Frank?"

"Yeah, but I got my own when I got kicked out. Why?"

"Did you get a new number?"

"No." Lee didn't bother asking 'why' again. "Is there a point to all these questions?"

"Yeah. Go ahead and get us a new hotel and a new SIM card for Lee. Text me our new hotel and we'll meet you there." Hanging up with Gracie, Saul extended his hand. "Give me your phone, babe. I'm going to turn off the *Find My iPhone* locator. It seems your brother contacted a few people and let them know where you are, probably by using the app. Gracie said there are a bunch of paparazzi downstairs now. We need to pack up and relocate. Management has agreed to sneak us out of the back."

Lee fumbled then dropped his phone in his rush to give it to Saul. Picking it up off the carpet, he punched in the code to unlock before handing it over.

"I never even thought about that," Lee admitted. "How could I be such an idiot?"

"It's one of those things you don't think about once it's set up and not a big deal in the grand scheme of things. At least it was at the end of the day. Let's get packed."

Forty-five minutes later found them meeting Gracie in the lobby of their new hotel. "I have you guys all checked in. Here are your keycards. I just went ahead and got Lee the latest iPhone and added him to your plan."

"You're a star, as usual, Gracie."

"Thank you so much, kind sir. Let's head up to your room and have a little chat, shall we?"

Lee stared at Gracie as they rode up in the elevator. "You didn't have to get me a new phone, Gracie."

Gracie scoffed. "Your phone is embarrassing, kid. What is that? A five? It's one step up from a flip phone. Consider it a gift from me to you."

"Why would you—?"

Saul interrupted Lee's question. "Say 'Thank you, Gracie.' It's a sign she likes you. Go with it."

"Thank you, Gracie," Lee parroted obediently. "I'm sure I'll love it, even if it wasn't necessary."

Gracie patted his chest. "It's the least I could do. I know this has been a lot for an introvert like you. Sauly here doesn't have a shy bone in his body. Never has. I never had to worry about him in interviews or the like." The elevator arrived at their floor and Gracie stepped out and headed down the hallway, Saul and Lee following behind her.

After entering the room, Saul and Lee set their bags aside and sat down on the couch in the seating area. Gracie sat across from them in one of the chairs. "I don't know how much you're going to like what I'm about to say, Lee, but I think you need to seriously consider a restraining order against your brother." She held up a hand to forestall any comments from him. "Your brother sold your location to the paparazzi and he wasn't even smart about it. He found out you were gone because he showed up at Everyone's Mechanic looking for you today. Nobody told him anything, except that you weren't there. My understanding is he wasn't very pleasant and made some threats to the garage. Kirk is getting a restraining order-no trespass thingie — and yes that's the technical term — against him for the garage, which should protect you while you're working, but we're all worried about the rest of the time."

Lee swallowed hard. "I'm shocked he would take things this far. Selling my location to people and making threats… I'm wondering what else is going on. It just seems a bit over the top, don't you think?"

"That's what we're worried about, babe. He left you alone for months and now all this. I get that he accepted a job he wasn't qualified to do and spent the deposit, but what did he spend the deposit on?"

"I couldn't begin to guess." Lee closed his eyes and took a moment to think hard. Opening his eyes, he looked first at Saul then at Gracie once he'd made a decision. "Go ahead, Gracie. Let them get started on the paperwork for a restraining order. I just want to live my life."

"Good boy." Gracie stood and came to kiss Lee on the top of the head. "I'll call Jeff and get right on that. I went ahead and ordered some dinner for you. It should be here shortly. Get some sleep afterward. Early day tomorrow. I'll meet you at the studio." Gracie left after bending down to kiss Saul's cheek.

Chapter Fourteen

Saul looked around for Lee before scanning the street for their car and driver, who was taking them to the interview. Six a.m. was a disgusting time to have to be out of bed, let alone have to be somewhere you had to be pleasant and smile at people. He was trying really hard not to growl at anyone, especially Lee. Mornings were *so* not his friend.

"Here, babe," Lee startled him as he suddenly appeared at his elbow.

Saul looked questioningly at Lee to see him holding out a to-go cup of coffee. "Where did you get that?"

Lee chuckled. "Didn't you notice the Starbucks next door? That's where I went when I told you I would be right back. Here. A venti americano—and I have a spare." Lee held up the second cup of coffee in his other hand to show him.

"I love you."

"Are you talking to me or the coffee," Lee asked with a smirk.

"Can it be both at the moment?" Saul sipped his coffee then just held the cup to his mouth, inhaling the coffee fumes. After a few more sips, he lowered the cup to look at his boyfriend. "Thank you."

"Not a big deal. It's just coffee."

"I didn't mean for the coffee."

"What did you mean then?"

"For being here with me. I know it's a lot."

"Partners, right?"

"Yeah." Reaching out, Saul took Lee's hand in his, just as the car finally pulled up to the curb. The driver hopped out and opened the door for them with a smile and a friendly "Good morning, sirs."

Saul grunted at him, released Lee's hand and climbed into the car as Lee chuckled and greeted the driver. "Don't mind him. He hasn't had enough coffee yet. We're working on it."

"Understood, sir. My wife is much the same."

Saul slid to the other side of the car and grabbed Lee's hand again once Lee was in, resting their clasped hands on his thigh, while continuing to sip his coffee. He'd finished the first and had just taken the second cup from Lee when the car eased to a stop at the curb. The driver opened the door a moment later.

"Here we go, gentlemen. I've been told you'll be done at about eleven-thirty. Here's my card. Call when you're almost ready. I'll come back to get you and take you to the airport. My understanding is you have a three-thirty flight. Is that correct?"

"Yes, it is."

"Is it okay to just leave our bags in the car?" Lee asked.

"Yes, sir. I'll take good care of them."

"Thank you."

"No problem, sir. It's my job, after all. Good luck today, gentlemen."

"Thank you." Saul steered Lee toward the entrance where they were greeted by Vera Iverson herself. She was currently wearing a T-shirt and jeans, a far cry from the designer dresses and pantsuits she usually wore on the show.

"Good morning, gentlemen. Saul, it's a pleasure to meet you — and you must be Lee." She hugged them both, squishing them all together. "I am so happy you chose my little show to be your official first interview. The buzz has been a-maaazing. Let me walk you back to hair and makeup. Is that what you're wearing?"

Saul looked down to check his custom-tailored Armani suit before looking back up at Vera. "Yes. It's what Gracie thought would be best."

A flicker of what could have been fear at the mention of Gracie crossed Vera's face. "It's a good choice. You look quite dapper. Now, walk with me, gentlemen."

Vera speed-walked down the hallway and through a secure door to the backstage area. After a lot of twists and turns, they finally stopped at a room with six chairs situated in front of brightly lit mirrors. Two of the chairs were already filled, one with an Olympic diver and the other with a tennis player. Greetings were exchanged all around as Saul was ushered into one of the remaining chairs and a cape was draped around his neck.

Lee was ushered to a chair nearby as Vera stood in front of Saul and leaned back against the table in front of Saul's mirror. "You will be last on the show today. It's only the three of you, so you'll each get a lot of camera time. Lee, I understand you don't want to be on camera. Is that correct?"

"Yes, ma'am. I'm only here for moral support."

"Pity. You're very pretty. The camera would love you."

Lee ducked his head in embarrassment.

"Leave him be, Vera. It's a big deal for him to even be here with me. One step at a time."

"If you insist. Let me know if you change your mind. On that note, I need to go get ready myself." With a final wave of her hand, Vera was out of the door.

Saul looked over at Lee to see he was looking a little wild-eyed. "Lee, why don't you get out your sketchpad. It always relaxes you. This makeup thing can take a while."

Lee looked happy to have some direction and reached for the satchel with his supplies in it. Saul had done some sports talk shows in the past and he knew it was a lot of hurry-up-and-wait and he'd encouraged Lee to bring it with him. Saul then relaxed into the makeup chair and let them do their thing.

They were all in the green room waiting for the show to start before Saul had a chance to check in with Lee again. Gracie had shown up about a half-hour before and had been prepping him for the interview. Lee contributed to the conversation every once in a while, but most of his attention was still on his drawing. The diver—Andy, he thought was his name—walked behind Lee's chair, glancing down at Lee's drawing before stopping and staring.

"That's amazing."

"What?" Lee asked as he spun around.

"That's amazing," he repeated, indicating Lee's drawing.

"Oh, thanks," Lee responded with a blush. "Just doodling. Here... If you want, you can have this one."

Lee flipped back a few pages in his sketchbook, tore out whatever was on that page and handed it to him.

Andy stared at the page a moment before staring up at the ceiling, obviously trying to get his emotions under control. "Wow. Hey, babe." Andy waved his boyfriend over from where he sat against the wall. Saul had been happy to see that Lee would have someone else to sit with during all this.

"What's up?"

"Look at this picture he drew of us."

"Wow. I'm speechless. That's amazing."

"May I see?" Saul asked, dying of curiosity.

Andy flipped the page around to show Saul the drawing of the moment Andy's boyfriend had come into the green room and leaned down to give Andy a kiss. The emotion portrayed in the sketch was incredible and so realistic that it seemed like they were going to step right off the page.

"Can you sign it? We'll have it framed." Andy handed the sketch back to Lee so he could scrawl his signature at the bottom. "Awesome. Thank you." Andy and the boyfriend, Steven-something, both reached out and hugged Lee at the same time. Saul chuckled at Lee's discomfort.

"You're going to have to get used to adoring fans, babe, if Gracie has anything to do with it."

Lee turned a glare on Saul. "What happened to one crisis at a time? I am *still* not discussing it yet."

Everyone laughed. "Oh, sweetie," the tennis player joined the conversation. "If Gracie has you in her sights, you might as well just give in gracefully now. She kind of has a reputation for getting what she wants."

"That may be," Lee replied, "but not today, Satan." Lee then made a cross with his fingers in Gracie's direction, laughing when she flipped him off.

"Well, you should think about it. This is really good."

Saul didn't particularly care for the way Steve's hand lingered on Lee's shoulder, but the show's theme music came through the speakers in the wall, catching everyone's attention before he could say anything.

Everything moved quickly after that, as first the diver then the tennis player left for the set. When it was finally his turn, Saul stood and gave Lee a peck on the lips and a quick hug before making his way to the door, turning back to give Lee a wink. A makeup artist gave him a quick once-over before letting him walk out.

The sense of calm he always got before a big event settled over him and Saul pulled on what his family called his 'game face' as he walked out. 'Never let them see you sweat' and all that.

Saul was greeted by a wave of applause, and after greeting Vera, he settled onto the couch. The time flew by as he answered Vera's questions about being gay and why he was coming out now. Gracie had prepped him well and everything went smoothly until the end, when Vera pulled up the Instagram picture he had posted of him and Lee.

"So, Saul, you have this gorgeous boyfriend."

"Yes, I'm very lucky."

"And he's here with you today."

Saul felt a frisson of alarm go down his spine. He did not like the look in Vera's eyes at all. He cautiously answered, "Yes, he's here to support me as I do this."

"I'm sure everyone here would just love to meet him, wouldn't you? Wouldn't you all love to meet Lee?" Vera asked, addressing the crowd. The crowd went into a frenzy of cat-calls and whoops, before finally starting a chant of "Lee! Lee! Lee!"

Saul tried very hard to keep his composure on-stage. He knew the camera was on him. He looked to where Gracie was standing just off-stage, at a loss for what to do. He knew what he wanted to do. He wanted to yell at Vera for putting him in that position then stomp off-stage, but he was a professional. He could do this. He stood and faced the crowd. Moving his arms up and down, palms down in the classic 'quiet' movement.

Glancing back over at Gracie, Saul saw that Lee had joined her, looking very concerned. Saul minutely shook his head in Lee's direction, hoping to convey that he didn't need Lee to come out. Saul turned back to face the crowd.

"Sorry, folks. Lee is mine and I'm not ready to share any more of him yet. As I told Vera before the show, he's shy and we're easing him into all this with baby steps." Saul gave a self-deprecating laugh before hamming it up a little for the crowd. "I am *not* easy. He has enough challenges right now." Saul got the laughter response he was seeking and turned to sit back down, shooting the still-seated Vera a dirty look while his back was to the camera.

Vera only flinched slightly before quickly resuming her professional demeanor. "Well, you can't blame a girl for trying, can you, Saul? I mean, look at him. He's gorgeous."

"I'm a very lucky man."

Saul managed to hang on to his composure long enough to finish the interview but got up and left the stage quickly as soon as the director yelled, "Clear." He had no fear Vera would be able to follow him, since she had to do the show wrap-up and get through Gracie. He met Gracie and Lee as he came off set.

"Let's get out of here. Do we have everything?"

"The only thing we brought extra was my satchel and I have it here. Gracie called the driver. He should already be waiting."

"Great. Let's go. I can wash off the makeup at the airport. I'm done."

Gracie hopped in with them as they made it to the car then it pulled away. "We have time, boys. I've instructed the driver to take us to my place so you can decompress a few minutes before you head to the airport. Right now, you look like you're ready to kill someone. It's probably not the best image to put out there, especially as you're traveling with Lee. People will say you're upset with him."

Saul closed his eyes and took a moment to calm himself, breathing in through his nose and out through his mouth, concentrating on finding his center. Opening his eyes, he looked at Lee sitting beside him. "Sorry about that. She had no right to try to do that to you. We were very clear."

Gracie grunted, drawing Saul's attention to where she sat on the other side of him, drumming her fingers on the leather armrest of the car. "Oh, she knew, and she will be hearing from me very shortly."

"Let us know if you need an alibi," Lee offered.

"Ha. Like they would ever be able to trace it back to me if I did."

Saul chuckled then looked back at Lee. "Did you enjoy the rest of the show, at least?"

Lee winced. "Sort of. I mean, it was neat to see what happens behind the scenes of the show. Between the makeup and the lighting, it was fascinating. I really liked Andy and Steven too, until…" Lee stopped to bite his lip, looking very nervous.

"Until?" Saul prompted.

"Once you were on stage, Steven kind of hit on me. He asked if I would be interested in a ménage with him and Andy. I told him I was with you and we were exclusive. He said it was a shame." Saul had to laugh at how scandalized Lee looked. "I mean, if that's what they're into, more power to them, but…" Lee ended in a shrug, obviously having no words to describe how he was feeling.

Saul leaned in to give Lee a kiss. "I didn't like the way Steven kept leering at you, but I had faith you could handle it."

"Well, clue *me* in next time. You know I don't pay attention to that stuff."

"Noted."

The conversation was cut off by the ringing of Gracie's phone. "What a shocker. Vera is calling me." Saul watched as Gracie hit the Ignore Call button four times in a row before they reached Gracie's house. Gracie finally accepted the call after she'd instructed Saul to "Go wash that shit off" in typical Gracie fashion. Saul grabbed the extra clothes he'd planned to change into at the airport as he listened to Gracie absolutely rip Vera apart as he made his way to the guest room shower.

Feeling refreshed afterward, he followed the voices to Gracie's kitchen, where Gracie and Lee were at the breakfast bar with sandwiches and chips in front of them. A third plate sat in front of an empty stool in the middle. Saul made his way there before sitting and taking a huge bite of his sandwich. Gracie and Lee left him in peace while he ate, for which he was thankful.

"Better?" Gracie asked once he'd taken the last bite.

"Yeah. You know I love your sandwiches, Gracie. Thank you."

"Want to know what I said to Vera?"

"I don't know. I heard some of it as I walked upstairs. Am I old enough to hear the rest?"

"I don't think *I* was old enough to hear it. I feel a little traumatized, to be honest." Lee's voice had Saul looking at him a little more closely, to see Lee's wide-eyed look of shock.

Saul had to laugh. "I've seen her in action before. Gracie can be scary."

"That's one word for it," Lee said with a shudder.

"Nobody messes with my boys," Gracie said decisively. "Now that you're put back together and calmer, let's get you to the airport. I'll keep you posted on responses once the show airs later today."

"Sounds good. Thank you for everything, Gracie. I don't know what I would do without you."

Gracie put her hand on Saul's cheek. "You have a great group of people surrounding you. You'll do fine. Now, get out of here. I have some more terror to rain down on people and I don't want to traumatize Lee any more than I already have." With a cackle, Gracie escorted them out of the door, waving to them from the front stoop.

"Okay, let's go catch a plane."

"Let's go home," Lee responded.

"Even better."

Chapter Fifteen

Life had settled back into routine quickly after the show. While there had been some protesting outside some of their stores, it had not lasted for very long. Lee was very thankful for that. While the stores and the garage had lost a few customers, most had stayed, and they had, in fact, gained quite a few new ones once people found out they were gay-friendly.

Frank had been served with the restraining order and Lee hadn't heard from him at all. He was sure that was helped by the fact that he had a new unlisted phone number, but still... He had to admit he was a little concerned, since it wasn't Frank's normal mode to let something go if he felt he'd been wronged. Lee just focused on doing his job and working on his relationship with Saul. That was all he could reasonably control, but part of him was waiting for the other shoe to drop.

The custom paintwork he'd done for Sergei had led to a ton of referrals, keeping Lee very busy at work. The day before, a guy had brought his bike from Florida for

Lee to do his paintwork. It was weird and wonderful at the same time. There was so much to do that Lee had stayed late to work on a couple of the projects, since Saul had one of his protective equipment classes tonight at the store and wouldn't be home anyway.

He stood and stretched, eyeing his latest paintwork with a critical eye. He was happy with how this one had turned out. A dragon wrapped around the fuel tank. The glittering paint made the dragon seem like it was alive. He cleaned his brushes and shut off the lights to the shop, re-engaging the alarm after he went through the door. Getting in his truck, he moved it to the other side of the gate and got out to lock it behind him when he felt an electric jolt go through his body, rendering him immobile. He couldn't move to put his hands out to catch himself when he fell backward. His head hit the pavement and everything went black.

* * * *

Lee woke up with a start, looking around at his surroundings. He had no idea where he was. Nothing looked familiar. He tried to sit up, only to realize his hands were tied to the bedframe he was lying on. He panicked a moment, trying to figure out what had happened, the adrenaline causing some of the fuzziness to fade. He'd left the shop. He'd been locking the gate, then what? *I was kidnapped*? That would explain him being tied to the bed.

Luckily, whoever had taken him had left his feet untied, so he was able to ease himself up until he was sitting against the headboard. He made the mistake of leaning his head back, only to find a spot sore enough to cause a wave of nausea that had him leaning over the edge of the bed as much as he could and vomiting over the side. His head throbbed in time with the beat of his heart and he had to take a moment to gather himself back together. Now that he was marginally more awake, he looked around again and realized he did recognize where he was being held. He was in his family's lake house on Lake Gaston.

"Frank! You bastard! What have you done?" Lee yelled out only to regret it when it sent another wave of pain through his aching head. It had the desired result, though, because he heard footsteps coming down the hallway then the door opened to Frank's smirking face.

"Now, now, Lee. You know darn good and well Mom and Dad were married all legal-like before I was born."

Lee scowled at Frank. "Let me go!"

"Not before I get what I want."

"And what's that? I'm not coming back to work for you and Dad. I'm happy where I am, so get over it. There's nothing I'm going to do for you."

Lee didn't like the look of evil that came over Frank's face and had about two seconds to brace himself before Frank strode across the floor and backhanded him to the face, forcing Lee's head to the side.

"This whole mess is your fault. You couldn't just do as you were told. Oh no. Now my life has gone to shit and it's all your doing." Frank yelled the last right in Lee's face before backing off abruptly and punching the wall. "I want to kill you so bad, but I need you. You're going to get me the money I need."

"Why do you need money still? I already took care of Sergei's paint job. He told me you'd worked out a payment plan."

"And how exactly am I supposed to make those payments? Dad fired me when he found out about the

Sergei thing, ya know. Kicked me out of the house too, when he caught me letting the paparazzi know where you were in New York. It doesn't matter anyway, because the five thousand I owe Sergei is nothing."

"What do you mean? Who else do you owe money to?"

"Not that it's any of your business, but I may be in to Antonio for a little bit."

"Antonio? You owe money to Antonio Vargas? Are you *stupid*?" Antonio Vargas was a drug lord wannabe in Raleigh, with a hair-trigger temper.

"No, not stupid…a drug addict, Lee. A drug addict who wants to live — and you're going to help me."

"How?"

"Well, let me rephrase. Your boyfriend is going to help me by paying the ransom I'm about to request. A cool million will be enough for me to pay off Antonio and get out of town."

"You're an idiot."

"And yet you're the one tied to the bed. Smile pretty." Frank then held up his phone and took a picture. "Proof of life and all that. Now, if you'll excuse me, I have a ransom text to send."

Lee stared at the slammed door in stunned disbelief for a few moments after Frank left. "What the ever-loving hell?" Lee pulled on the ropes tying him to each of the bedposts. To his shock, the left one gave a little bit. Turning his head to examine the knot, he realized his brother had knotted it too close to the metal bracket supporting the bed. The rope was fraying every time he pulled on it. Lee kept an ear out for his brother while focusing all his energy on getting the rope to fray even more without making too much noise or motion. If he moved too much, his head let him know it with a massive wave of pain and nausea.

"Focus, Lee. You can do this," he whispered to himself. "You're bigger than him. You're definitely smarter than him. You have a great boyfriend." The last thought motivated Lee to try harder as he heard his brother coming back down the hall. The rope gave with a snap just before his brother came through the door. Lee shoved his hand back down toward the mattress in the hopes that Frank wouldn't notice he was almost free.

"Well, that was a nice chat. Your boyfriend sure wasn't happy to hear from me." Frank's laughter was slightly unhinged, making Lee take a closer look at him. His pupils were blown, and he was weaving on his feet a little bit. "They all think you're so special. You were always Mom's little angel, her beautiful little boy. Wonder what she would say if she knew you were a filthy queer?"

"She knew." That made Frank pause.

"What?"

"I told her before she died. She knew. She still loved me. She didn't care. Her brother was gay."

"You lie." Frank took a menacing step toward Lee, pausing when his phone started to ring. "I've got to take this. Don't go anywhere." Frank laughed his way out of the door.

As soon as he left, Lee went to work on his right hand. Once he was free, he stood, wobbling for a moment before looking around for some sort of weapon. To his shock, he saw his phone and wallet sitting on top of the tall dresser on the other side of the room. He moved as quietly as he could to pick them up before looking out of the window.

As he had suspected, he was in one of the upstairs bedrooms. If he wasn't injured, he probably could have dropped down to the roof of the front porch then from there to the ground. In his current state, there was no way he felt steady enough to attempt such a maneuver. Lee closed his eyes for a moment as another wave of dizziness hit. He definitely had a concussion.

Remembering the phone in his hand, he raised it to squint at the screen after unlocking it with his thumb. After a moment, he finally figured out the correct buttons to call Saul.

"Lee! Lee! Is that you?" The shouted words were like little bullets to Lee's brain.

"Shhhh. Not so loud. My head hurts."

"We saw Frank zap you on the security cameras. You hit the ground pretty hard when you fell, so I'm sure your head does hurt. Are you safe?"

"Not yet, no. I'm free from where he had me tied to the bed, though. We're at the family lake house on Lake Gaston. Can you come get me?"

"We're almost there, babe. Your brother didn't turn off his location app and the police were able to trace where you are. Just hold on. Where are you exactly?"

"I'm in the upstairs master. There's only one way out. My head hurts." Lee looked around for a moment, trying to remember what he was supposed to be doing.

"You said that, babe. I'm assuming your brother isn't in there with you right now."

"Nope. He got a phone call he had to take." Lee started to giggle. Man, maybe he was more hurt than he thought.

"Yeah, the police are on the phone with him negotiating the drop-off. Can you at least lock the door?"

"Yep. Yep. Yep." Another giggle. "Hey, Saul, I think I'm broken."

"We'll be there soon, babe, and get you all fixed up. Okay?"

"Okie-dokie. What was I doing?"

"You were locking the door."

"Oh yeah." Lee made his way over to the door just as it opened and Frank came through. "Uh-oh. Frank's here. Gotta go." Lee tried to put his phone in his pocket but missed and it hit the floor.

"How did you get free? Who were you talking to?" Frank yelled the words as he stomped toward Lee. Lee tried hard to focus and stood up as tall as he could. When Frank went to grab his shirt-front, Lee was able to grab his wrist and hold on to it. He was lucky he picked the correct hand coming at him, since he was seeing two of everything.

Lee then raised his knee and nailed Frank in the balls, making him double over in pain. Using the wrist still in his hand, Lee applied pressure and shoved his brother's arm behind his back then shoved Frank face-first up against the wall with a thud that jarred his already throbbing head. He pressed all his weight against Frank as another wave of nausea coursed through him.

Thankfully, before Frank could retaliate, a wave of people came through the door — or maybe it was just three. It was hard to tell at this point. Someone eased Lee away from Frank before taking over and zip-tying Frank's hands together. He vaguely heard Saul's voice coming from somewhere before the darkness rose up to take him again.

* * * *

Lee woke with a gasp what could have been minutes or hours later, sitting up in bed before having to grab his head in pain. He realized that he once again had no idea where he was or how he had gotten there. The last thing he remembered was the cavalry arriving. Looking blearily at his left arm, he realized he was hooked up to an IV. Hands appeared in his peripheral vision and Lee jumped again, yelping when it not only jarred his head this time but pulled on the tape for the IV.

"Easy, babe. It's me." Saul's soothing voice finally penetrated his panic after a few moments.

"Saul?"

"Yeah, I'm here."

"Where's 'here'?"

"The hospital, babe. You have a pretty nasty concussion. You need to lie back and relax. Let me push the button for the nurse. We've been waiting for you to wake up. You scared the shit out of me."

"I'm sorry?" Lee wasn't exactly sure what he should be sorry for, but obviously something was wrong if he was in the hospital.

"Nothing to be sorry for, babe. I put all of this firmly at Frank's door."

"Frank? Am I going to be okay? Why am I here?"

"Please calm down. It's going to be okay. You're here because you have a concussion and the place where the barbs hit you got a little infected. Do you remember Frank kidnapping you?"

Lee had to think hard. Bits and pieces finally coming back. "Yeah. Frank needed money. He hurt me." Lee's eyes closed again, now that the adrenaline rush had ebbed. He was so tired and Saul was here, so he was safe. He would just close his eyes for a few more minutes.

Chapter Sixteen

Saul leaned against the back of the elevator in the hospital, allowing the exhaustion to consume him for a moment. It had been a horrible three days. First, discovering Lee was missing, followed by phone calls from Frank. Seeing the security camera footage of Frank coming up behind Lee, tasering him and watching Lee hit the pavement would haunt him for the rest of his life. Luckily, a drug-addled person was not the best planner or they might have been in serious trouble.

As it was, Lee had been diagnosed with a pretty nasty concussion and an infection from where Frank had just yanked the barbs out of Lee's back, but there were no brain bleeds, so at least they were lucky in that regard. Any movement of Lee's head or light caused Lee a lot of pain and nausea the first couple of days, though, and the doctors had decided it was best to monitor him in the hospital for a few extra days.

Saul had haunted the hospital as much as they had allowed him to be there, but he wanted to take his boyfriend home. He really needed Lee to be in their home and in their bed where he could hold him and reassure himself that Lee really was okay. Saul was met by a very cranky Lee when he walked through the door, who at least had some color in his cheeks and looked better, even mad.

"When are they going to let me out of here? I need to sleep, and these people won't let me."

Saul gave him a weary smile. "Don't pout, love. They said maybe today but probably tomorrow. You have to be able to drink without vomiting, otherwise you'll get dehydrated and end up right back here." Saul leaned down to give him a kiss. "Hi, by the way."

"Hi. Sorry. I'm cranky. I haven't vomited at all today and they took out my IV. I want to go home."

"And I want you there, babe, but not if it compromises your recovery."

Lee sighed long and loud before leaning back in his hospital bed and taking a good look at Saul. "You look worse than I do. You should go home and take a nap. One of us should be able to get a good night's sleep, at least."

"I'll try to sleep tonight. It's been a little crazy."

"What's going on?"

Saul hesitated. "Your brother was killed last night at the prison where they were holding him."

Lee gasped. "Oh no. But I guess that's not exactly surprising, considering who he owed money to."

"No, it's not. He was still your brother, though."

"Yeah. How's Dad doing with it?"

Surprisingly that had been the one positive to come out of everything. Lee's dad had shown up at the hospital, frantically asking to see Lee. Saul had not been inclined to let him, but Mama had stepped in and pulled Mr. Clark aside to speak to him. After passing the Mama test, it had been decided to let him in to see Lee, but Saul was not at the point where he trusted him to be with Lee alone, not until Lee was back on his feet and maybe not even then.

"Your dad was sad, of course, but he seemed resigned to it all. The press has been going crazy with all this. It's been a challenge to dodge the news people. Gracie and Jeff are working on it."

"They've had to work on a lot of stuff together of late. Is Jeff going to be number five?"

Saul chuckled. "It's possible. Jeff was wearing a very fetching shade of lipstick yesterday." Lee's laughter eased something in his chest.

"Hey, what's wrong?"

"Why do you think something's wrong?"

"Because you're crying," Lee said, waving at Saul's face.

Saul raised his hand to his cheek and was surprised to find tears. "I didn't realize. I'm so happy to hear you laughing again. I was worried for a while there that I wouldn't."

"Oh, babe, come here." Lee held out his arms to Saul, waving his hands in a 'come' motion to get him to move.

Saul sat down on the bed and allowed Lee to pull him close. Laying his head on Lee's shoulder, he let it all go. "Sorry. I'm just so very tired."

"It's all good. I'm going to be okay. Frank is gone and can't hurt us anymore. I have my dad back in my life. Things are looking up." Lee used his hand to raise Saul's head to look him in the eye. "And I've got *you*. If I've got you, all the rest is just gravy. You're part of my foundation. I love you."

"I love you too…so much. I was so scared…but then we got there to rescue you and you had already rescued yourself."

"I obviously wasn't going to stay conscious for much longer. I was very happy that the cavalry arrived when it did."

"Me too, love." Saul pecked Lee on the lips before leaning his head back onto Lee's shoulder. Lee tightened his arm around him for a moment. Saul relaxed and gave him his weight as Lee raised one hand to start petting the back of Saul's head.

Saul was startled when the doctor came through the door. "I hear someone's ready to leave us."

Saul stood and moved away as the doctor made his way to the bed to check out his patient. Saul rubbed his hands over his face, trying to focus through his exhaustion. He looked at Lee and was happy to see a smile on his face as he chatted with the doctor. Saul stepped into the bathroom to splash water on his face, returning in time to hear the doctor say Lee could go home.

"Really? Today?" Lee lit up when he got the doctor's nod. "You hear that, Saul? I finally get to go home."

The doctor teased him back gently. "Now, now, son. Keep it up and I will begin to think you didn't like our hospitality."

"You all were excellent, but this isn't home, and I think this guy has been running himself ragged trying to see me."

"I would agree." Turning to address Saul, he said, "You are under doctor's orders to take a few days off and hang out with your boyfriend. You both need rest."

"Yes, sir."

"Don't make me call your mama, Saul."

"She's Mama," Saul answered with a shrug. "She already knows."

The doctor left and Saul went to grab the duffel bag of clothing he'd brought for Lee to change into.

"As sexy as the hospital gown is, babe, how about we get you dressed and ready to go. Hopefully, the nurses will be in shortly so we can go."

Shortly turned out to be overly optimistic. They had plenty of time to get Lee changed then the waiting game began. Saul used the time to take trips to the car with the things Lee had accumulated in his hospital room over the last couple of days. He transferred balloons from the guys and little girls, flowers from his mama, greeting cards and the duffel bag of clothes to the car.

A phone conversation with Mama helped distract Lee for a short while, but after that, Saul was hard-pressed to keep Lee calm during the wait. He was ready to go and ready to go right then. Saul was certainly looking forward to Lee being home and he couldn't wait to have Lee sleeping in his arms once more.

Finally, the nurse came in with the discharge papers and a wheelchair to take Lee to the car.

"I can walk," Lee grumbled.

"Hospital policy, babe. The sooner you let them wheel you out of here, the sooner we can get home. Let me run ahead and grab the car." Saul leaned down to peck Lee on the lips before grabbing Lee's remaining duffel bag and the plant his sister and her family had sent to Lee, before turning and striding out of the hospital room and into the elevator.

By the time they made it back to the apartment three hours after seeing the doctor, Lee was pale and shaky again. Saul had tried to avoid as many bumps in the road as he could during the ride, but it had been impossible to miss them all. Hell, the hospital parking lot had speed bumps every fifty feet.

Lee was not a silent sufferer. "Why did it take three hours from the time the doctor said I could go home until now?"

"I don't know, babe. Hospital bureaucracy sucks."

A few moments later, "Sorry."

"I know you are, babe. You've been through a lot. Let's get you upstairs."

Saul went around and helped Lee out of his SUV and got them headed in the direction of the door and stairs to the apartment. It was very slow going.

"Maybe I should consider having an elevator put in." Saul huffed as he was carrying most of Lee's weight by the time they made it to the top of the stairs.

"Bet you're sorry you ever met me, huh?"

"Where the hell did that come from?" Saul propped Lee a bit against the wall so he could unlock the front door.

"It's just that I've brought nothing but drama, almost from the start."

"Let's get you to the bedroom before I drop you. We can discuss this later."

"Sorry."

"And stop saying sorry! You have nothing to be sorry for!" Opening the door, he grabbed hold of Lee again and they made their slow progress to the bedroom. Sitting Lee on the bed, Saul removed his shoes and socks. "We're probably going to have visitors. Are you comfortable enough in your sweats and T-shirt?"

"Yeah, I'm good. Much better than the hospital gown."

"Okay, good. Think you can get yourself under the covers while I grab you a bottle of water?"

"Yeah, I got it."

"Okay. Be right back." Saul used the time he was grabbing the bottles of water to calm down. After a few minutes he felt ready to talk to Lee in a calm manner. Returning to the bedroom, he was surprised to find Lee already asleep. "Guess the talk will have to wait. He has the right idea, though." Changing quickly into his own sweats and T-shirt, Saul climbed into bed with his boyfriend before easing him into his arms, happy to have him back where he belonged.

* * * *

Saul woke with a start to find Lee climbing back into bed. "You should have woken me."

"I had to pee, and you looked so peaceful sleeping that I hated to do it. I will ask you for help in the shower in a little bit, though. I need to get the hospital smell off me."

Saul pulled Lee back into his arms with Lee's head resting on Saul's chest. Saul rubbed Lee's back first over Lee's T-shirt then sliding his hand under it, being careful to avoid the bandage covering where the barbs had been imbedded. He needed to feel his boyfriend and know he was really there.

"You okay?" Lee whispered.

"You scared me. I don't think I've ever been so scared as when I saw the security footage."

"But I'm here now."

"You're here now." Saul tightened his arms around Lee for a moment. "What was that bullshit about regretting meeting you earlier?"

"It was bullshit. I was tired and feeling overwhelmed. I love you."

"And you know I love you too."

"I do. It's what got me through the kidnapping and these last couple of days at the hospital." They were both quiet for a few moments. "Did you see the news vans in front of the store?"

"I did. You had to figure they would be there, though, with your brother being killed last night."

"Yeah, I guess." Lee paused. "I didn't want him to die. I mean, I'm not surprised, since he was dealing with some pretty dangerous people, but I didn't want him to die. I wanted him to get help."

"I know you did, babe, because you have a big heart. I'm not sure there was any saving him, though. He didn't want to be saved."

"I know. I'm thankful for his part in helping us find each other. I don't think I ever would have met you if I'd continued to work for my dad."

"That's true and a good way to look at it. I am so thankful to have you in my life. I love you."

"You are the touchstone of my life and the cornerstone for the rest of the foundation we have yet to build together." Lee leaned up to give Saul a gentle kiss. "Hopefully that's all the earthquakes for a while."

Saul had to laugh. "Yeah, let's hope for no more earthquakes."

"Let's take another nap before your family gets here."

"Good idea. Nap then shower then just living happily ever after."

But Lee was already asleep and didn't respond.

Epilogue

"I can't believe you brought me to Paris for our one-year anniversary as a couple. This is amazing." Lee stared out of their hotel window at their view of the Eiffel Tower. He couldn't wait to go up in it. Saul's arms came around him from behind.

"I thought you would like it. We'll head to the Eiffel Tower in a little bit then grab some dinner before coming back for an early night. That's probably all we'll feel up for with the jet lag."

"I can get behind that plan. When do you want to head out?"

"In a minute. I need to do something else first," Saul said while stepping back and to Lee's side.

"Oh, what's that?" Lee asked, glancing over to Saul, just in time to see him go down on one knee. Lee gasped and raised his hand to his mouth in shock.

Saul raised an open jewelry box toward Lee with two titanium bands inside. "Lee, you are the love of my life and I can't imagine my life without you in it. Will you please marry me?"

"Yes. Of course, yes!" Lee joined Saul on his knees on the floor, raining kisses all over his face.

"Here," Saul said gruffly. "Let's see how I did in guessing the size." Saul then took Lee's hand and one of the rings out of the box and slid it onto his left ring finger.

"Perfect fit. Now you." Lee grabbed the second ring and slid it on Saul's left ring finger before raising his hand to his lips and kissing the band. "Perfect."

Lee leaned in and kissed Saul, and as usually happened between them, one kiss became two then three. Before Lee knew it, they were writhing naked on the bed until they were a sweaty mess, covered in their combined releases.

Lee lazily pressed a kiss over Saul's heart before rolling to his back to hold his hand up and examine the ring on his finger.

Saul smirked at him. "Does this work as a private, romantic way to ask you to marry me?"

"This was perfect. I had no idea. You hadn't mentioned it in a while."

"You didn't really think I'd changed my mind, did you?" The smile slid off Saul's face.

"No. We're solid. I know we're solid. After seeing how crazy Eric and Kirk's wedding planning went, I figured maybe a wedding wasn't so important."

"Yeah. I guess that's what happens when you involve two little girls in the planning. I thought the horse-drawn carriage from the wedding to the reception was an interesting touch and I loved the kites they had you paint with scenes from their castle. Fred the dragon was magnificent in flight." They both chuckled. "It was also interesting to see the sparks between Stuart and Sergei."

"I know, right? I wonder if anything will come of it?"

"Who knows. Please say you don't want to have a huge wedding like that, though. I'll be happy to go to a justice of the peace and be married."

"Me too. Quiet and simple. I just want to be able to call you my husband."

Saul exhaled a sigh of relief. "We'll apply for the license when we get home."

"Sounds like a plan. All I need is you, although maybe we should let Mama plan a reception or something for us or she'll be upset."

"What happened to the rule of not talking about Mama while in bed?"

"True. That can wait for later. In the meantime, fiancé" — Lee rolled back on top of Saul and began kissing him — "we can see the Eiffel Tower tomorrow."

Want to see more like this?
Here's a taster for you to enjoy!

Linchpin
Jodi Payne

Excerpt

Randall Quinn's new ride was pretty sweet.

The BMW was fully loaded, including an in-dash navigation system, Bluetooth fucking everything, and a black leather and wood grain interior. She was comfortable and stylish, and her engine vibrated gently but powerfully, like a wild cat getting ready to pounce. *Mrowr.* Quinn tapped a button on the dashboard display and practically summoned up Zeppelin with the power of his fucking mind. Damn, the technology gods were good. He sped down the rural highway, *Black Dog* sinking straight into his psyche through the seven-speaker surround sound. Fuck yeah.

His new baby was paid for in full, and in cash. He'd finally laid by enough in savings that he could afford to spend with more freedom. He'd never gone in for such an extravagance before, but he'd been salivating over this baby at the dealership for a month and he'd eventually broken down and done it. She was a hot-red color — well, the dealership called it something stupid like Orange Metallic, but it was basically red — which, admittedly, didn't fly under the radar the way she probably ought to, but Quinn didn't care anymore. After over ten years in the biz, he'd fucking earned the right to show off.

He'd pulled in that stack of cash on a high-end hotel assignment he'd had a week ago. Swanky, several-thousand-dollar-a-night hotel suites were always a challenge, but this one was even more so than usual and had definitely warranted the boost in pay. The boys had made a royal mess of the place, so much so that Quinn figured they must have had some seriously specific and scary fucking orders. There'd been blood and fingerprints everywhere and Quinn had had to deal with stains in the carpet, on the wallpaper, and splattered across furniture. Even with a crew, the cleanup had been a pain in the ass and had taken almost two full days. He'd even had to replace the carpet and a fucking couch.

It was damn lucrative as far as such things went, to be sure, but Quinn had sat in a bar for a couple of hours alone afterward, and he and his bourbon had decided it was about time to call it quits. Quinn was coming up on thirty-nine and he was getting a little old for this shit. He'd kind of fallen into this line of work back in his twenties when he'd made his daily bread working for the coroner's office and cleaned up crime scenes legally. It hadn't been long before a particularly influential lover had shown him where the real money was, and Quinn had found himself literally seduced into a darker world by the fine art of cleanup to cover up.

"Aaaaaand, here we are." This job wasn't going to be as big a payday, but smaller gigs like this were simpler, and made up more of his bread and butter. He pulled into the motel parking lot, waving a hand across the display to mute the radio. So. Fucking. Cool. Slowly, Quinn drove along the length of the building until he found room three-twenty-nine. The location was perfect, way down at one end and on the first floor. Easy in, easy out. Seemed those muscle boys were finally learning. He turned around and headed back to the main entrance.

Quinn touched a button on the display and the sound of a ringing phone filled the interior.

"Found it?" a familiar voice answered — a fucking party in the sack.

"Hey, sweet cheeks."

"Seriously, Randy? What did I tell you about work, man?"

Quinn laughed. Mikey had a lickable ass, but the rest of him didn't interest Quinn much. "I'm here."

"Got it. You're on the clock."

"Do I have resources?"

"Boss says he already cut the manager in. The boys told him you wouldn't need a crew."

"Did they, now? And what the hell do they know about it?" Seriously, you give someone a few too many steroids and put a gun in their hands, and they suddenly think they know everything. Those muscle boys were big and dangerous, no question, but they were dumber than a sack of hammers. Their combined IQ wouldn't buy you a cup of coffee. Quinn, on the other hand, was an artist. What the boys did took brawn. His job was far more delicate. It required a keen mind and fastidious attention to detail. What could he say? It was hard to be humble.

"Make sure you talk to Davis. The room's paid up for two days."

"Perfect." Unless those boys chopped their target into little pieces or pulled another Jackson Pollock, two days was more than enough time to set this derelict flophouse to rights. "I'll check in again in an hour or so."

"Later." Mikey hung up.

Surveying the premises from the parking lot didn't improve Quinn's assessment one bit. This place was the very definition of shithole. The roof was warped, the siding moldy, and the main office wasn't really an office at all — it was just a glass window with a fucking pass-through. Chances were good he was looking at bulletproof glass, too. Classy. He took note of the surveillance camera over the window as well.

Erring on the side of caution, Quinn left the car running and the driver's side door open. He knocked on the thick glass, summoning a small man with greasy hair, dirty fingernails and a cigarette hanging from his mouth.

He squinted at Quinn. "Yeah?"

"I'm here for three-twenty-nine."

The guy nodded. "Heard you was comin'. I'm Davis." He slipped a key into the pass-through.

Quinn shook his head. "I'm not touching that. You let me in."

Davis sighed. "I don't want nothin' to do with nothin'."

"You wanna keep that paycheck?" Quinn asked, pulling his Beretta off his hip and holding it flat against the glass. "Or see what's behind door number two?"

Davis sighed. "Right." He took the key and disappeared back into the office, appearing again in the breezeway.

Quinn nodded and got back in his car. He'd be damned if he was going to let his baby out of his sight. He drove her down the length of the building again and parked outside room number three-twenty-nine, then pulled his kit off the front seat and got out of the car. "Don't go anywhere, beautiful," he said, polishing a fingerprint off the driver's side door. Yep. Pretty sweet ride.

While he waited for Davis to catch up, he dropped his kit on the concrete slab outside the motel room door and took out a pair of latex gloves. After pulling them on with practiced ease, he tugged his gun from his belt again.

"I'm coming, I'm coming!" Davis called nervously, picking up his pace. He'd gotten the wrong idea, but Quinn was fine with that if it lit a fire under his ass. Davis put the key in and hastily unlocked the motel room door.

"Thank you," Quinn said, tapping the gun against his thigh for effect. "Now. The surveillance camera – "

"Hasn't worked in years. It's not even hooked up to anything. I just keep it there so people think – "

"Fine. You can go now."

Davis turned and hurried back into the office.

Quinn chuckled. This really was a great location. If Davis stayed nervously respectful, his motel could see some repeat business. Davis could even make enough money to put some lipstick on this pig.

The metal door to number three-twenty-nine looked as though it had been kicked in more than once in its lifetime. The jamb was bent, the doorknob sat at a bit of an angle and rust had eaten through the olive paint in several places. Quinn gave the knob a turn and it protested weakly, but then the door swung away from him.

He held his gun up near his face, sighting down the barrel as he scanned the room. Satisfied, he put the piece back in his belt and went inside, closing and locking the door behind him. The motel room was a pit.

The bed was hollow, the drapes hung unevenly and were a hideous shit brown, and the carpet was industrial, worn with the traffic of many feet, and looked like vomit. He noted the older model TV, a tall lamp in one corner and a ragged-looking lounge chair underneath that. He squinted at what he supposed was meant to be art hanging on the wall over the bed. He sure saw a lot of fucking shit in this room.

What he did not see was a body.

With a shake of his head, he moved to the closet and pulled it open. Nada. He figured that the target must be in the bathroom, which was certainly considerate of the boys, as it was much easier to wash away the evidence in there. He stepped through the bathroom door and turned on the light.

"Mmr!"

Quinn's eyes flew open wide. "What the fuck?"

PUBLISHING

Sign up for our newsletter and find out about all our romance book releases, eBook sales and promotions, sneak peeks and FREE romance books!

About the Author

Ann Marie James is fluent in two languages, English and sarcasm. She believes that you will never learn anything new if you don't read as much as you can, and/or talk to every stranger you meet. She always looks for the best in people and to treat people the way she wants to be treated. Above all Ann Marie believes in love, whatever form it takes. Relationships are hard, love is the glue that keeps it together.

Ann Marie loves to hear from readers. You can find her contact information, website details and author profile page at https://www.pride-publishing.com

www.ingramcontent.com/pod-product-compliance
Lightning Source LLC
Chambersburg PA
CBHW020416180626
46812CB00003B/1010